P9-CNI-712

CALL ME FLOY

JOANNA COOKE

YOSEMITE CONSERVANCY | YOSEMITE NATIONAL PARK

Yosemite is pronounced "yoh-SEM-ih-tee."

yosemite.org

Yosemite Conservancy inspires people to support projects and programs that preserve Yosemite and enrich the visitor experience.

Library of Congress Cataloging-in-Publication Data

Names: Cooke, Joanna, 1975- author.
Title: Call me Floy / Joanna Cooke.
Description: [Yosemite National Park, California] : Yosemite Conservancy, [2020] | Audience: Ages 9 to 12. | Audience: Grades 4-6. | Summary: Floy Hutchings, nearly twelve, struggles against the expectations of 1876 society as she fights to protect her beloved Yosemite Valley and dreams of climbing Half Dome. Includes tips for visiting wild areas and historical note.
Identifiers: LCCN 2019053558 (print) | LCCN 2019053559 (ebook) | ISBN 9781930238992 (hardback) | ISBN 9781951179038 (epub)
Subjects: CYAC: Sex role--Fiction. | Family life--California--Fiction. | Grandmothers--Fiction. | Indians of North America--California--Fiction. | Yosemite Valley (Calif.)--History--19th century--Fiction. | California--History--19th century--Fiction.
Classification: LCC PZ7.1.C64753 Cal 2020 (print) | LCC PZ7.1.C64753 (ebook) | DDC [Fic]--dc23
LC record available at https://lccn.loc.gov/2019053558
LC ebook record available at https://lccn.loc.gov/2019053559

Cover art by Zeke Peña
Book design by Melissa Brown
Map by Gary Bullock
Manufactured using recycled paper from sustainable sources.

Printed in Canada
1 2 3 4 5 6 – 23 22 21 20

To all young people:
Go write your own story.

YOSEMITE VALLEY, 1876
HALF DOME
NEVADA FALL
SNOW'S
MIRROR LAKE
VERNAL FALL
GLACIER POINT
ILLILOUETTE FALL
ROYAL ARCHES
YOSEMITE FALLS
SALLY ANN'S VILLAGE
SENTINEL DOME
IDA'S CLASSROOM
HUTCHINGS CABIN
HUTCHINGS HOTEL
COSMOPOLITAN
LEIDIG'S HOTEL
GLACIER POINT TRAIL
FOLSOM'S BRIDGE
EL CAPITAN
MERCED RIVER
CATHEDRAL ROCKS
EL CAPITAN MEADOW
E
N
S
W
BRIDAL VEIL FALL
BIG OAK FLAT ROAD

NOT MANY PEOPLE, let alone a girl my age, can say they are the heroine in a real novel. The book was published when I was only eight years old, and I am just shy of twelve now. But being cast as a heroine has been worse than scrubbing Grandmother's underthings. When people meet me, they expect the girl from the novel. Her nickname was "Squirrel," just as mine once was. And she is mischievous, like I am prone to be. But I am not her.

I am Florence Hutchings, and you may call me Floy.

ONE

If there's one thing to know about me, it's that I do not like walls.

Specifically, the walls of Mrs. Pinkerton's classroom, where I sit now. She stands at the chalkboard, with her back to the class. My younger sister, Cosie, sits next to me, hands folded, listening like the good girl she is. I have long since ceased paying attention, but the last words I remember Mrs. Pinkerton saying are, "Never forget to cross your *t*'s. An uncrossed *t* is just an *l*." Perhaps she has moved onto arithmetic now.

I wouldn't know.

My eyes trace a path along the pipe of the woodstove, as I slide into my imagination. There I am, completing the first ascent of the most iconic mountain in my former home of Yosemite—Half Dome. For as long as I can remember, I've wondered how one might climb to its top. Half Dome rises into the sky like a roll of bread cut in two. A sheer face and rounded curves polished to a mirrorlike sheen. Climbing such a peak is impossible! Yet just last autumn, Mr. George Anderson scaled the mountain's eastern side, drilling bolts into the rock and climbing to the top.

How did he manage it? Was he not scared?

More than one visitor to Father's Hutchings Hotel endured my tales about completing the climb, but only a fool would have believed me then. I was six! After telling the tale often enough, I surely felt as if I *had* climbed the mighty Half Dome. Now, in my imaginary climb up the stovepipe, I do not falter. My feet step firmly on the smooth granite, and my grip on the rope is unwavering. I have almost reached the summit, with Clouds Rest and the glaciated peaks beyond, when Cosie shifts loudly in her seat, and my eyes open.

Drat.

The walls around me are not granite and moss-covered but wood-paneled and decorated with the alphabet.

Cosie's eyes are glued to the front, her pencil hovering over her workbook. Mrs. Pinkerton has just begun writing out a long exercise for us to copy, handwriting being critical to our development as capable citizens. This process will take her a while. Who could stand another minute of such drudgery? My gaze turns toward the window and the gray sky of San Francisco above.

I'm not one to pass up an opportunity.

I reach out and touch Cosie's elbow. She turns to me, eyebrows pinched in concentration. I tip my head toward the door, and her eyes widen. She does not say it's a bad idea, though it always is. Instead, Cosie waves me off encouragingly. I hold her gaze a second longer in thanks—she'll take my books home like she always does—and then slip from my chair and out the door.

I run.

The road is packed hard beneath my feet, and my knees ache. Never did my body hurt during my explorations in Yosemite. There I could hop from boulder to granite boulder, ascend rugged trails, and splash across creeks without a moment's discomfort. But San Francisco is absolutely unforgiving in every way. The air smells of coal-fire smoke and horse manure. I must dodge through crowds of people. All stare at me as I push past. There aren't even any trees to line my way!

Life in the city threatens the soul.

When I have finally run far enough, I slow to a leisurely stroll. This is not my first escape—nor will it be my last.

At Pine Street, I turn right toward the docks, instead of left toward Grandmother's boardinghouse. Mother will likely be absent, fussing over some new artist friend as usual. And Father—he'll have his nose pressed against another one of his magazine articles, proofreading the final version before printing. So there is little for me at Grandmother's, save a lecture from her. She shall be furious to learn I've skipped out of school again.

Third time this week!

Soon the salt of the bay stings my nose, and I pull my skirt up at the knees and begin to run again. At last I find a street lined with budding trees. City houses all look the same to me, but ask me to identify one of the sparse trees in San Francisco and I can name them all. That skill comes from Mother. For all her artistic sensibilities, the woman loves plants. I touch the trunks as I move past. Alder, locust, oak. Truly, there are too few.

Oh, to run as far as Yosemite!

I would gladly shout out the names of the thousands of trees lining that valley, if only it would mean I could stay there forever.

Ahead loom the piers of the San Francisco harbor where Russian sailors haul cargo off merchant ships just in from the Pacific. Disappointed miners drift along the docks, searching for boats to return them to cities in the East. Rows of steam ferries line up to transport travelers across the bay and up the Sacramento River. My eyes settle on one named *El Capitan*. Was the ferry named for the towering rock at the mouth of Yosemite Valley? Either way, seeing the words on the ship's bow sends my thoughts into the mountains, and a plan begins to form in my mind. When we lived in Yosemite, I moved about as I wished, wandering the open forests and sleeping under the stars. I know the way back like a compass knows north.

If the mountains are where I wish to be, then what am I waiting for?

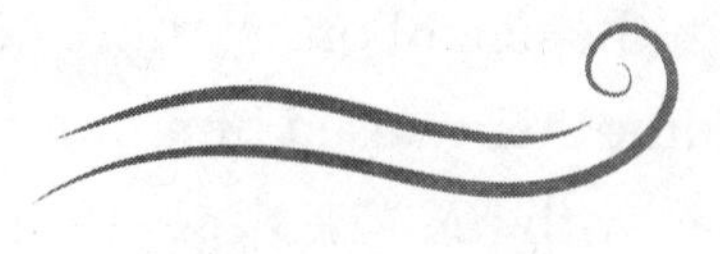

TWO

Grandmother's boardinghouse bustles with preparations for supper when I finally arrive. All but one of the rooms have been rented to the usual crowd of boarders, sea captains. They can be rowdy at times, but Grandmother runs a tight ship and at this hour will be overseeing her kitchen staff. Thirty minutes remain before the evening meal—just enough time for me to collect what I need and sneak out. I move quickly through the foyer in hopes of getting to the stairs unnoticed and make it all the way to the third-floor landing before a small voice behind me says, "Where are you going?"

I stop, my foot in midair. *William.* I must play this moment perfectly, lest he repeats what I say and ruins everything. "Hello, Willie," I say as I turn.

My six-year-old brother stands a few steps up from the last landing. His knee-high socks show the telltale signs that he played in the neighbor's manure heap again, and I wonder if Grandmother refused him lunch for it.

"Florence, stay with me," he begs. Although he's reaching toward me, his crooked spine makes him appear as if he's caught in a perpetual turn.

Was I muttering to myself as I'd climbed the stairs? How can he know what I'm planning? Tonight, I leave this place. The cramped streets with no place to roam, the idleness of school and home, the dresses that must be kept clean, and the curls that must be perfect—all of it will soon be behind me. I'm leaving for Yosemite.

Unless Willie gets in the way. Poor boy doesn't mean it, but this isn't the first plan of mine he's interrupted.

Willie shifts, trying in vain to straighten out his uneven shoulders. "Floy, it's simply boring at home. Maybe you could stay at home with me instead!"

"Blazes," I whisper. My own shoulders drop—that was close.

His eyes widen. "Don't let Grandmother hear you talking like that again."

I cackle in a most unladylike manner. "Oh, Willie!"

He's right, of course. Only yesterday Grandmother refused *me* my dinner when I laughed at the way one of her guests called Yosemite quaint. There is simply nothing quaint about the towering cliffs and misting falls of my home! Besides, Grandmother would have a bigger objection to what I'm planning than to my swearing or rudeness. I only have to make sure she doesn't find me out until I'm long gone.

My hand slips inside my apron pocket, and my fingers brush against a crusty biscuit left over from my midday meal. "Would you like this?"

Willie takes the biscuit eagerly. It's a rare treat, given Mother's insistence that we consume mostly fruit. He gobbles the biscuit down, crumbs catching on his shirt. I stifle the urge to wrap my arms around him.

Drat.

I will miss him when I leave, even if he is the world's most maddening little brother. Well, Cosie can play nursemaid to him. Grandmother's voice climbs the stairs as she barks orders in the kitchen, and the moment passes. It's time for me to go.

I make for the stairs, but Willie catches the hem of my dress with his stubby fingers.

"Let go, Willie. I'm . . . just going to get you something special."

He releases me. "All right."

Taking the stairs two at a time, I make it to the cramped room I share with my siblings. Hidden underneath my mattress is a wooden cigar box. It holds a favorite Yosemite treasure as well as all the money I've amassed over years of picking up loose coins. Truly, the people who rent rooms from Grandmother—or did from Father when we lived in Yosemite—should be more careful. I hope it will be enough for my travels. The stairs creak underneath someone's footsteps.

"William James Hutchings!" I shove the coins into my pocket, pressing them against the remnant biscuit crumbs. "It's a surprise, so no peeking!"

"Florence, you know I do not enjoy surprises."

I freeze. *Grandmother.*

Cosie, whose real name is Gertrude, was named after the ship Father sailed on from England. How impressive! At least Father insisted I be called Florence, instead of Florantha after my grandmother. Holding the box against my chest, I take a deep breath and turn around.

Grandmother scowls down at me. Her appearance could be regal, with her crisply ironed dress and excellent posture, if not for the full jowls resting on the collar of her dress. She looks like a bulldog in women's clothing!

I instinctively straighten and run a hand over my tangled curls, my insides boiling at her effect on me. "I was just . . ."

Her scowl deepens. "You ran from school today. Again."

Because of Willie—my dearest, blessed brother—I am ready for her. "I had to run home to get this surprise ready for William." I hold up the box and shake it. My treasure, the granite chunk I'd found on our last ride out of Yosemite, rattles within. A slim excuse, but it's all I've got to go with.

"Mrs. Pinkerton sent a boy."

Now it is my turn to scowl. It's always the boys who are sent on errands. Could've been Timothy McDoughal—he's the fastest boy in our class. I, however, can cross the city faster than everyone at school, because I'm not afraid of using dark alleyways and streets filled with drifters. Has Mrs. Pinkerton ever sent me? Not a once.

"Quit frowning, Florence. How many times have I told you—"

"The wrinkles will stay," I finish for her. For all the lines crisscrossing her face, it's a wonder she has the nerve to admonish me at all.

She grunts, then begins pacing. "Schooling for a lady is of the utmost importance," she starts, when a door slams from down below. Heated voices rise from the first floor, and she closes her eyes. "We will continue this conversation later. For now, your father would like to speak with you."

A lump forms in my throat.

Father is the last person I want to see right now, because if one person has Yosemite on the mind more than me, it's him, and that is a dangerous thing. What if he senses my plan? What if he forbids me to return?

Avoiding him isn't an option. I follow Grandmother back down the stairs, the cigar box tucked under my arm. When Grandmother stops on the landing to steer Willie back to his room—such conversations are not for young ears, she tells him—I continue on, each step feeling as if it's one more in the wrong direction. One more step away from my reunion with Yosemite. The anticipation of leaving has built up so much, it must be released. I stop on the bottom stair and spy a place where Grandmother's new wallpaper has peeled free from its glue. I reach out and yank the paper away from the wall. The silk tears underneath my fingers in a satisfying rip.

Man alive! That felt good.

I practically skip the last few feet to the study, where Father's voice carries through the closed door. He's talking to someone, too quietly to be understood through the door, but his tone is quite familiar. He's exacerbated, and a smile plays at my mouth.

One of the few times it's not me tormenting him!

As I listen, something else familiar makes me pause—a discontented sighing after every burst of speech from Father's mouth. Mother is in there with him. Turns out I was wrong.

Father is *not* the last person I'd like to see.

Mother has been disappearing more and more often to attend services at the Swedenborgian Church. She claims it's for the artistic freedoms offered there, but mostly it seems she is avoiding us. It's been well over two weeks since my last glimpse of her. Why is she here? I press my ear to the door.

"She knew I was too young," Mother says. Her voice

trembles. "And the twenty years between you and me is too much. I cannot bear it anymore."

"Do not speak to me of what you cannot bear," Father replies, his voice thrumming with tension. "And do not speak to me of *him*."

Right as I'm starting to piece their conversation together, Mother begins using hushed tones. I step away from the door and close my eyes. It's clear enough that Mother has formed a close bond with someone, someone who is not Father.

The little opening I felt in my heart thanks to Willie's charm snaps closed.

I've often thought that Mother seems to tolerate me, Cosie, and Willie, rather than love us. Our family has already endured Father's legal battles over his Yosemite property, and the scrutiny is wearing on us all. Could it be a good thing if she and Father lived apart? My hands ball into fists at my sides.

To be unburdened by the whims of others!

To be free!

My eyes fly open, and I am more determined than ever. I *will* leave for Yosemite and escape this madness.

Today's plan has been foiled—tomorrow will have to suffice. I shall depart for school as always and take Hansen Street all the way to the pier. From there, the ferry sails eastward toward Oakland and the trains that can carry me closer to the mountains beyond. If anyone tries to make me return home, I'll use my reputation—as Father's mischievous daughter, as the girl from the novel—to convince them that returning to Yosemite is exactly what he's asked me to do.

Now that I think about it, it's a wonder it's taken me so long to come to this plan.

I knock on the study door and enter.

THREE

Mother stands forlornly at the window. Seeing her strong nose, long black curls, and deep-set eyes is a bit like looking into a mirror. Even her sad expression seems the twin of the one I likely wore today while dreaming of Half Dome. Nevertheless, Mother barely glances in my direction. Devils to her, then.

I turn to Father. He's sitting in the chair he crafted from manzanita wood—a chair that I find neither comfortable nor handsome. At the sight of me, his mouth turns down at the corners. I recall Grandmother's admonishment about wrinkles, though I dare not repeat it to him now.

"You asked to see me?" I say.

"Sit," he replies.

My body tenses. Father's usually not this short with me.

"I can explain," I start, daring to hope that the same excuse I'd given to my grandmother will work with him, too.

He holds up a hand. "No. This involves your grandmother. We shall wait for her."

I move to the sofa across from Mother. Her face remains positively fraught, and she pulls nervously at the end of one of her curls. While Father fusses with lighting his pipe, I open my cigar box and take out my chunk of granite. I begin counting the dark specks embedded in larger pink and white crystals, when the room goes strangely quiet. I look up. Father is staring at the rock in my fingers.

I hold out the coarse stone. "I found it on Black's drift fence near the bottom of El Capitan," I say. "The day we left."

When his eyes meet mine, they are filled with sorrow. After ten years of fighting for his right to own property in Yosemite, he was evicted from the very place he'd made famous, from his home. It was my home, too.

"Yes, well," he says. "Put it away."

I look down at my hand. Does he mean I should actually put the rock away? Or is he speaking of Yosemite? I don't really want to know what he means. I return the rock to the cigar box and place the box next to me on the sofa.

It feels like a month of Sundays before Grandmother strides in, a beaming Cosie in tow. My sister crosses the room, and Mother wraps a limp arm around her shoulder, offering a bland smile. Cosie is innocent enough to eat it up.

Father clears his throat and takes his pipe from his mouth. The family is now present—minus Willie—so he can begin.

"Our departure from Yosemite last fall came with more uncertainty than on other occasions that we have left for the winter. No doubt this continues to weigh heavily on all of us," he says, speaking of his eviction. "The strain has affected some more than others." He looks pointedly at me. I resist the urge to slump into my seat and instead sit a little taller.

Father strides across the room to a painting he commissioned on his first trip to Yosemite. It shows the towering rock walls on each side of the Valley, the lazy Merced River snaking through the Valley's center, and the peaks beyond. His gaze traces the image, as if searching for something hidden. With his magazine and illustrated talks, Father has done more to share news of Yosemite than any other. He's barely spared a thought to anything else since I was born.

Father turns back to us. "I've done too much to promote the Valley to let it go so easily. And in a week's time, I shall return."

Perhaps I should wash out my ears as Grandmother suggests, for I cannot believe Father's words. Has my dream come true so easily?

"My hotel has been sold, of course," he says, "but I shall work as a guide."

"Now, James," Grandmother says, just as I cannot contain myself any longer.

I leap from the sofa, cross the room to Father, and wrap my arms around his thin frame. "Thank you, Father. Thank you."

Rarely have I hugged my father in this way, and he gently puts his hands on my shoulders and peels me free. Holding me at a distance, he meets my gaze. "Florence, my girl, what's come over you?"

"I am so happy to be returning."

"You misunderstand. You will not be joining me."

I take a step back. "Father, I . . ."

He turns his back to me, a clear dismissal.

I continue retreating until my legs hit the sofa and I flop down. My mouth opens, but I am stunned into a rare silence. How could Father even consider going without me? I'm about to say as much when Grandmother speaks up again.

"A week is quite soon, James," she says, redirecting the conversation back to the logistics. "I trust you've already made arrangements, then?"

Cosie leaves Mother's side and sits next to me. Even though I'm older by a year, she looks out for me, just as she does Willie. She reaches for my hand and taps a finger against my pinkie. I tap back, glad that at least *she* can see how unfair this is.

Father draws from his pipe, smoke billowing around

his face. "For some weeks, I've been communicating with George Leidig, and Mr. Snow as well. They've made arrangements for . . ."

Just as with Mrs. Pinkerton's lectures, I stop listening.

I cannot bear it that his dream is coming true as my hopes are dashed. I look to the painting of Yosemite, my eyes falling on the hazy hint of Half Dome in the background. There will be no chance now of making my own way to the Valley. With only a handful of hotels—all run by his dear friends—Father would surely find out if I were there.

All at once, the hope in my heart is replaced with outrage. Father was born in England and traveled across the country to reach California. Yosemite is but one of his adventures. All I have is Yosemite. I was born there. And it's the only place I ever want to live.

How can he deny me that?

I jump to my feet. "Why?"

Father turns from Grandmother. "Come now, child, I should think you know. How many times have you run from school since our arrival—seventeen? Twenty? We've only been here five months!"

"It's no secret why I abandon school. I want to return to Yosemite as much as you. Why won't you take me with you?"

"This is why," he says, gesturing to me.

"I don't understand."

"It's your impertinence, Florence."

Impertinence? Does he mean me speaking my mind? I've been doing that since the day I was born.

"I won't be able to attend to you," he says. "I shall be writing a new edition to my guidebook and also plan to lead trips. Some to Half Dome, if all goes well. I've written to Mr. Anderson for—"

"You . . . you plan to climb Half Dome?"

When he nods, I sit back down. This time when Cosie taps my finger, I do not tap hers in return.

The desire in Father's expression—the desire for Half Dome—is plain as day, but there is something else in him, too. I glance at the bookshelf behind him, overflowing with titles on all subjects. There, exactly where I expect it to be, rests the green spine of that dreadful book, *Zanita: A Tale of the Yosemite*. Gooseflesh trickles up my spine. Could Father's desire for Half Dome be as mine is—tainted with fear? No, the tightening under Father's eyes is envy. Someone has gotten to the prize before he could. I felt the same way when I found out about Mr. Anderson's feat.

Robbed.

And now Father's going to be the second person to rob me of Half Dome, and there's nothing I can do about it.

FOUR

Cosie taps my finger until I look at her. She's studying my face, likely wondering what plan I'm concocting. I always have one. Except for now. Cosie regards me with pity in her eyes, and my heart sinks. I tap her finger once, and then look away.

Father has moved on from lecturing me, and he now stands at the window opposite Mother. Her tense, clasped hands do not make sense. Shouldn't she be happy that he is leaving San Francisco and putting distance between them?

"James," she says, "what of . . ." She glances toward the sofa where Cosie and I sit. If Father leaves, then she will be stuck with us.

"Indeed," says Grandmother. "What of the children?"

I scowl, not caring if Grandmother sees. Father will

return to his beloved Yosemite. My beloved Yosemite. *Our* beloved Yosemite. Cosie and Willie both miss the sweet scent of the ponderosa pines and clear mountain air, as I do. Given the chance, we would all return.

"Yes, what of us?" I interject.

"Florence, at least, should go with you," Grandmother says. "The city does not suit her."

Father does not answer right away, and the air in the study seems to thicken as we wait for his response.

"I cannot attend to her," he repeats.

I straighten in my seat. "Since when have I required attending?" I ask. "I shall be quite independent, as always if you think about it, and I won't talk to you at all, if that's what you want."

"The Valley school must be reopening soon," Grandmother adds.

Last year, Father and the other residents had successfully petitioned the Mariposa County Board of Supervisors for the development of a school. All summer, Mr. Chestnutwood taught arithmetic and history to twenty-two students perched on a log with a view of Yosemite Falls. My daydreaming was far easier to accomplish there than in Mrs. Pinkerton's room. Regardless, school is not part of my plan.

It never is.

Though I would surely endure it, if it allows me to return to my mountains.

I glance at Cosie, wondering what she thinks of this proposal of separation. Aside from my regular wanderings, we've never really been apart. Will she think it unfair that Grandmother suggested that only I accompany Father? This time I initiate the tapping, and Cosie taps back immediately.

"If Florence attends school—without any attempts to run away or cause trouble—then I will allow her to return with me," Father says.

I jump up. "Yes, thank you, Father!"

He waves me off and begins stroking his long beard. Though I know this means he's not quite finished, my joy cannot be diminished. Never mind the arrangement Grandmother and Father have made about my attending school. Or that somehow, he thinks I might not venture off on my own explorations. As soon as I return to my Valley home, life will be what it was.

I shall climb trees and splash in the mighty Merced River and lie in the grass underneath the darkest of skies.

Blazes! I am Yosemite bound!

"Florence," Father says, "sit down." He waits until I'm once again seated next to Cosie before continuing. "About this trip, there are a few other arrangements . . ."

I shift closer to my sister. "Cos," I whisper, "I can hardly believe it. I'm going *home.*"

She swats at my nose. "You're insufferable," she says quietly. "It's not as if we hadn't left Yosemite before."

"This time was different."

Every other time we'd left for the winter, we had a plan to return. But last fall, we departed in a cloud of uncertainty. Years have passed since the State of California determined that Father's claim to the land was not valid. But he fought the decision and refused to leave. The sheriff finally evicted him last year. Would Father's removal be permanent? We'd all thought as much, even though Father had vowed to come back to the Valley. Why had I ever doubted him? He's as stubborn as I am.

My eyes dart to the hazy mountain at the back of the painting. *Half Dome.* The rendering does little justice to the peak, tucked beneath clouds and overshadowed by El Capitan and Bridal Veil Fall in the foreground. I've seen it from enough angles to know its magnificence regardless.

Half Dome is an altar to the stars and heavens above, and I must find a way to climb it, despite everything. If I don't reach the top, something might always be missing inside me.

Cosie elbows me in the side, and I jerk my attention back to the conversation. Grandmother is addressing my father. "What you ask of me, James, is simply not possible."

I lean toward Cosie's ear. "What did I miss?"

Cosie whispers, "Father has insisted that Grandmother come as your chaperone."

"Chaperone?" I say, too loudly. All eyes fall on me. Even Mother glances my way. I clear my throat and say, as calmly as I can muster, "I have no need of a chaperone."

Father's hand drops from his beard. "Not before," he says, "but you are becoming a young lady and should act as such."

Young lady?

I slouch against the sofa. Proper manners be gone, I want nothing to do with young ladies! If I were a boy, I wouldn't need a chaperone, and Father would surely let me accompany him on his climb. Then Cosie nudges me a second time, and I realize I've missed something important again.

"I cannot leave the boardinghouse for one child," Grandmother is saying. "And heaven knows, Gertrude and William will need looking after." She first glances toward Cosie and then looks at her daughter, who is still standing miserably by the window.

Mother straightens her waistcoat in an attempt to appear steady, but her shaking voice betrays her. "I am leaving. I cannot endure this any longer."

I snort. It's as if she's taken the words right from my mouth.

She pauses at the door, her gaze skimming over me to land on Cosie. "Daughters, I am sorry."

Her eyes are set—she means to leave for good. Mother disliked living in Yosemite, her strange diets were frowned upon by many, and she never knew what to do with me. I will not miss her too much. Cosie is a different matter.

Next to me, her body tenses. Even if she'd heard the rumors, she never would imagine that Mother would simply leave. I take Cosie's hand in mine. Neither Father nor Grandmother says anything as Mother marches into the hall, silence hanging over the room until the front door snicks shut.

Father sets down his pipe, rubs his face with both hands, and drops into a chair.

Grandmother clicks her tongue. "That, while not surprising, complicates the situation." She addresses Cosie and me and waves a hand in the direction of the door. "Wash up now. It's time for supper."

That is all she has to say about her daughter's departure! "What of Cosie and Willie? And of me?"

Father takes a long draw from his pipe and holds his mother-in-law's eye for a moment. Then he turns back to me. "I suppose the three of you had better start packing. We're headed to Yosemite."

FIVE

In the days that follow, I can barely contain myself. When a letter must be sent, I offer to take it to the Wells, Fargo and Company office down on Montgomery Street. When Father's new boots are ready to be picked up from the cordwainer's shop, I'm out the door with nary a word. Eventually, tired of finding jobs for me to do, Grandmother sends me off to my room, where the idleness spins my mind. Yosemite is on the horizon, and Half Dome is in my sight. What will happen when we arrive?

Now, standing on the platform in the bustling town of Oakland and awaiting the 12:14 train to Niles, my enthusiasm erupts from me like Yosemite Falls in springtime. I am pacing and tossing my granite chunk in the air, closing my eyes at the last second and trying to catch the rock blinded. It's my eleventh failure in as many attempts, but I am not deterred.

"Floy," Cosie says wearily from her perch on our baggage. "Could you please hold still for one second?"

Willie sleeps against her shoulder. How can either of them possibly be so tired at a time such as this? Cosie did bear the brunt of my frenzy over the last few days, but still.

"How can you be sitting down? The train's expected in"—I glance at the overhead clock—"two short minutes, and then we shall finally be on our way!"

She doesn't mention that we've been on our way since last night, when we caught the ferry from San Francisco to Oakland. Nor does she bring up the three days of travel—by train, stagecoach, and horseback—still ahead of us. She yawns and says, "I've made this journey as many times as you have, Floy."

I toss my rock into the air again. Cosie has no idea that Half Dome is on my mind. The need to tell her tugs at me, but I worry the words will choke me.

A whistle blows in the distance, and Willie snaps awake. By the time the train pulls in a few minutes later, steam billowing around the engine, Cosie and Willie are standing at my side. She gestures with her head for me to move closer to the track. It's a silent challenge I cannot refuse. I salute her and step to the edge, wanting to feel the push of air as the engine rolls past. Heat from the steam stings the skin on my neck, but I do not twitch. The cars coast by, not even an arm's length in front of my face, and I lift my hand as if to trace a line down the side of the train as it moves past. Then a hand clamps onto my shoulder and hauls me back.

"Florence," Grandmother says, her voice like a leash, tugging me into line.

Grandmother could not be less thrilled about leaving her boardinghouse and has informed me, on more than one occasion, that if I do not meet her expectations, I risk the lot of us being sent back to San Francisco.

We board the Alameda Valley line to Niles, where we change to the Western Pacific. This train, part of the newly completed Transcontinental Railroad, is bound for Promontory Summit, Utah, but we will disembark long before then. Cosie pulls out a map Father has given her of that route and entertains Willie by pointing out sites of interest. But nothing beyond the granite cañons of my beloved Sierra Nevada matters to me, and I press my face against the window. The train shudders across the bridge over Alameda Creek, and the boulders below create a jumbled cascade for the bubbling water, so akin to the racing creeks of Yosemite. We ride deeper into the rugged cliffs of Niles Cañon, and my restlessness begins anew.

The train reaches the wheat fields of the San Joaquin Valley and pulls into Stockton station by suppertime. We find lodging at the railroad hotel, already humming with travelers en route to places like the lake at Tahoe,

Los Angeles, and, of course, Yosemite. Not a single child is in tow, and so Cosie, Willie, and I cause quite the stir as we gather for the stages in the morning. Once people hear we grew up in Yosemite, questions abound. I am happy to oblige the curious travelers after days of having my enthusiasm for our return quelled by my family. Luckily, Grandmother is too busy with dealing with the luggage to notice the small crowd that's formed around me and cannot keep me from embracing this opportunity.

"I am fond of saying that Yosemite and I are the same age," I state loudly so that those craning their necks at the back can hear. "You see, I was born in 1864, and this was also the year that President Abraham Lincoln protected the Valley, as well as the Mariposa Grove of Big Trees, for all to see their shining glory, for years and years to come. In fact, I'm returning to celebrate our twelfth birthdays together!"

Cosie snickers beside me, for that's hardly our reason for returning. Even Father chuckles. If anyone's shown me the value of a good story, it's him.

"And Mr. Muir," a woman calls out, "have you met him?"

Father's chuckle fades, but I will not let him ruin my fun. Little does he know I secretly read the articles John Muir published last year in the *Overland Monthly* magazine, and finer words about the Sierra and the wonders of Yosemite have never been written.

"Met Mr. Muir?" I say. "Indeed, it's fair to say he raised me!"

Like the birthday party, this is also a convenient half-truth. When Mother insisted we subsist on fruit and alfalfa, Mr. Muir made sure to share his fresh milk and bread with first Cosie and me, and Willie, too, once he'd come along. Nearly five years have passed since Mr. Muir fell out of favor with Father, but I do not mention this to the crowd. "Mr. Muir was a frequent companion on my adventures through the Valley, and I daresay I taught him everything I know."

The crowd laughs. Since our abrupt departure last year, I have not felt as alive as I do now, pulling memory after memory from my mind for my rapt audience. I am about to continue, but the horses are hitched and ready. Grandmother leads me, Cosie, and Willie to the first stagecoach and directs us up the step. The four of us squeeze onto the slimly padded forward-facing seat. Father sits opposite us, in the backward-facing seat, next to a lawyer from Virginia, who is headed to Yosemite as we are.

Never one to pass on a chance to tell his story, Father explains his claim. "I bought my hotel in 1864. We moved in six weeks before the United States government granted Yosemite Valley to the State of California. You can see my predicament. I was clearly living there first."

"And you made improvements to the property?" asks the lawyer, Mr. Tomlinson.

"I built trails and roads. By our cabin, there was a five-acre farm, complete with a sizable strawberry patch, with which to serve the tourists. An apple orchard for pressed cider and pies."

Grandmother chimes in. "My daughter and I planted those trees."

"And I ate the strawberries!" I add. It's too early for them to be fruiting now, but the thought of their sweetness makes my mouth water.

Mr. Tomlinson laughs and then turns back to Father. "Your claim seems reasonable enough. And still the courts decided against you?"

"The California courts voted in my favor, but the United States Supreme Court did not. We were forced to leave."

The lawyer tips his head thoughtfully. "Still, Lincoln did a rare thing in protecting Yosemite. And during the war, no less."

When the conversation turns to the newly created national park at Yellowstone, I look away, grateful for a window seat. California in springtime is surprisingly green. The rolling hills are dotted with fragrant wildflowers, and Spanish ranches offer wide expanses for cattle to range free. The occasional grove of fig or olive trees offers inviting shade. It's a pastoral prelude to the dramatic scenery awaiting us, and my foot taps out an impatient beat against the wall of the stage.

The hours drag on, with a few stops to change the teams,

but finally the foothills steepen, and the horses strain up the graded road to the mining town of Chinese Camp and the Garrett House. We disembark and slap our hands against our clothes to release billowing clouds of dust from the long day's travel. Cosie leads a sleepy Willie inside the dining room, and I follow. Inside, a slate sign advertises pot pie with pan bread for twenty-five cents. My stomach growls, and not for the first time I'm glad that Mother isn't here to deny us these tasty vittles.

We sit, and the mistress of the establishment slides plates in front of each of us.

"Eat up, then," she says, then heads into the kitchen for more plates as Father, Grandmother, and the lawyer from Virginia sit at a nearby table.

"Cosie," Willie says, his mouth full of bread, "will I go to school with you?"

I think back to him expressing the same sentiment on the stairs at home. What would have happened had he not intercepted me? Might I be in Yosemite already? I take a slow bite of the salty pie, unsure if that would have been better than these events.

"Don't talk with your mouth full, Willie," Cosie says gently. "And no, you're too young, I think. Last year Mr. Chestnutwood only allowed students over the age of seven."

Willie hangs his head. "I want to go to school, too."

I reach over to pat his hand only to realize the poor boy

has fallen asleep! Cosie and I quickly mop our plates clean with the pan bread. Then, cradling Willie against me, I follow Cosie up the stairs to our room for the night.

The sun is barely cresting the horizon when the first travelers mount their mules for the trip to Sonora and the gold mines beyond. When I'd asked to ride alongside our stage, Father had refused. He had even brought up that term *young lady.* Now he is engaging some travelers freshly returned from the Valley, while I wait impatiently under an oak tree for our stage to be ready.

Cosie and Willie join me in the shadows. "Don't worry, Willie," Cosie is telling him. "You'll have all the Leidig children to play with. Maybe you can help care for their chickens."

"But will *you* play with me?" he asks, rubbing his eyes. He flops down at the base of the tree and begins collecting acorns.

"I'm going to school with Delia," says Cosie. With her finger, she traces shapes on the bark. Only when she hands him a perfectly horse-shaped piece of bark does his face lift. Satisfied, she turns to me. "Floy, who are you excited to see?"

I think about her question. Certainly not Delia, though she and Cosie always got along. Johnny Boitano was always game for an adventure. And Sally Ann. We'd played together when we were younger, until the arrival of more tourists meant the Indians had to stay farther apart from us. Mostly, I'm just excited to see the mountains. I turn to Cosie. "You are referring to people?"

She pokes me in the side. "Of course I mean people. You cannot tell me that the only things you've missed from the Valley are the boulders and jays."

"That is precisely what I miss, Cos, and you know it well!"

"I do." She smiles, then her brow pinches. "Truly, Floy. You've been a miserable rot since we left last year." I'm about to protest, but she waggles a finger at me. "Do not deny it. You've a plan. I can see it in your eyes."

My breath snags in my throat. Here is my chance!

I glance at Willie and, seeing him sufficiently occupied with making tidy rows of acorns in a clearing of dirt, lean closer to Cosie. "I hope to climb Half Dome." The words feel fierce and impossible in my mouth—it's the first time I've uttered them aloud in months—but my heart swells with hope. "I shall find a way to join one of Father's parties."

Cosie pulls back, her eyes wide, and I'm plunged into doubt.

"You think me foolish?"

She shakes her head. "I know you, Floy. I can see why you would want to climb Half Dome. I only wonder why you haven't attempted it on your own already!"

Suddenly even this shady spot is too hot. Cosie is right—climbing Half Dome alone is exactly the kind of thing I *would* do, and still the thought of it makes my stomach turn. Her steady gaze weighs on me. I take a deep breath. "Do you remember *Zanita*?"

"How could I forget?" she replies. "Mrs. Yelverton's novel. Zanita is the girl that she based on you."

"Do you recall how Zanita died?"

She pauses. "No."

"She falls from the top of a cliff. From the top of Half Dome."

Cosie reaches for my hand, and I am glad that she is the nice sister, here to comfort me as she always comforts Willie. "Floy, it's just a story. You know Mrs. Yelverton had a flair for drama."

What she doesn't say is that I, too, have a flair for drama. And a tragic death sometimes feels like a certainty.

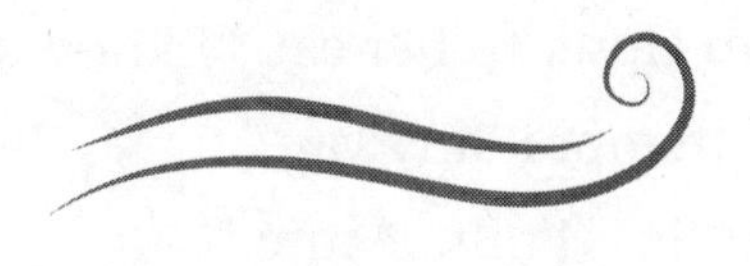

SIX

Father calls to alert us that the stagecoach is ready, and Cosie tugs Willie to his feet. It's his turn by the window. Wedged between Cosie and Grandmother, I am forced to stare at the stage wall between Father and Mr. Tomlinson. The stage bumps along the Big Oak Flat Road, and I lift my kerchief over my mouth. It's meant to keep the dust away, but I want to cover my entire face with it. What was I doing telling Cosie about my Half Dome dream? Why did I fill our heads with a vision of me falling from the summit?

Cosie leans her head against my shoulder. "I'm sorry about that wretched book."

I lift my kerchief a little higher on my face. Grandmother

snores on my other side, and Father is debating legal matters with Mr. Tomlinson. No one is paying us any attention. I lean closer to her ear. "I know what you'd say. That I should attempt it anyway."

She bites her lip. "I'm not sure."

A flutter dances in my stomach. Always Cosie's encouraged me in our adventures. Except Half Dome is something else entirely, and I need her to believe in me. To believe I can accomplish this. "I've scaled other peaks with Father before," I start, but then Grandmother stirs, and my mouth snaps shut.

Cosie changes the subject, wondering aloud whether she would finally be taller than Delia. Willie claims the first thing he is going to do upon our arrival is catch stone flies in the Merced River. When Mr. Tomlinson asks about our childhood in Yosemite, Father eagerly describes life as one of the first settlers in the Valley, second only to James Lamon. I don't remind him that Awani people had lived there first. All that matters to Father is the idea that he and Mr. Lamon pioneered life—and tourism—in Yosemite, and Mr. Tomlinson eats up his story.

Just a story.

Cosie's words stick with me for the rest of the day's journey. Not until the stage has climbed the steep grade into the grove of giant sequoias at Crane Flat do Cosie and I get a chance to talk again.

The stage stops to allow the other travelers to explore

the mammoth trees, and I scan the forest for the sequoia's distinctive red bark, counting more than two dozen giants. Cosie and I pick our way through patchy snow to investigate a downed sequoia, broken into large pieces by its fall. The old, gnarled roots extend higher upward than the height of the stage, and we crawl into an alcove under them. The moist air of our hideaway cools my skin—a welcome change from the heat and dust of the road—and my nose fills with the sweet scent of earth.

I'm nearly home.

Cosie leans her head against my shoulder. "I didn't mean to doubt you. I didn't mean you couldn't do it."

"I know Zanita's not real," I say, sliding my hand across the smooth, bare roots of the ancient tree. "But doesn't it seem uncanny that she died doing the one thing I want more than anything?"

"Tell me again. She fell?"

I shake my head. "They found her body in Mirror Lake and surmised that she'd been pushed from the summit. See? It all seems so real, or at least possible."

Cosie shivers and says, "If you must go, go alone."

"Why?"

"That way no one can push you."

She holds my gaze for a moment, and then we burst out laughing.

I wipe my eyes. "I needed that."

"Gertrude!" Grandmother's voice rings out. "Florence!"

Cosie jumps up and offers me her hand, but I gaze at the majestic trees a few seconds longer before letting her pull me up. Then we retrace our steps through the budding dogwoods and wild azaleas until we reach the Tunnel Tree. Earlier this spring, a massive hole was sawed through the base of this fire-scarred sequoia, allowing the stages to pass through. As Cosie and I pass through the opening hand in hand, I wonder at the rightness of such a choice. Even blackened and destroyed by flames, this tree is nothing short of miraculous.

Inside the tunnel, Cosie tugs me to a stop. "Just be careful," she whispers. "On Half Dome."

"I shall try."

What else can I say?

Grandmother waves us over to the stagecoach, where Willie is fast asleep and snoring on the bench seat. We climb back in, waking him up enough to stretch him out over our laps. Then the stage starts up the last climb toward the small outpost at Crane Flat, where we'll make a short stop.

The road offers glimpses of open meadow, and already there are cows nibbling at patches of new grass. Ahead lie Gobin's Hotel and the saloon run by Billy Hurst. Father will head directly for Gobin's for refreshments, but it's Billy's place that I love. It's where all the sheepherders and mountain men come to restock and to drink. It's a raucous, foul-mouthed atmosphere compared with the warm hospitality of Gobin's. Decidedly unfit for young ladies—and therefore perfect for me.

The stage jerks to a stop. While Grandmother fusses with a sleepy Willie, I climb out and race to Billy's. Shouts and rough laughter boom through the open doorway, and I cannot step inside fast enough.

Billy raises a hand to me from behind the bar. "Well, Floy! It's about time we saw you again." He is the only adult I know who calls me by my preferred name.

I pass a table of men playing pinochle and climb onto one of the stools. My mouth hurts, I'm smiling so hard. "Man alive, Billy! It's only been five months, but you look ancient!"

He howls with laughter. "I've only just opened for the spring. How will I look by the end of the season?"

Billy's saloon is only a few years old, and each year we stop by on our way to and from San Francisco. When Father carted us back to the city on what I thought might be my last trip, Billy cheered me up by telling me rude jokes and teaching me how to cheat the mountain men at cribbage.

I point to a bear skull on the shelf behind him. "That's new." Then a faint but decidedly putrid odor hits me. "And a bit smelly!"

"A grizzly wandered through the meadow a month ago, and you can imagine how well that went over with

Mrs. Gobin. We made quick work of him, but maybe the skull needs a bit more cleaning."

"You think so?" My laughter is drowned out by that of the cardplayers. "What else did I miss?"

He sets a glass of milk in front of me. "A whole lotta nothing and just 'bout everything. Don't let me start on all the new hoity-toity tourists at the Cosmopolitan Saloon in the Valley."

I savor my milk as he talks, ignoring the fact that the stage will soon be ready to go. At first, it's just Billy's voice that soothes me, but the more he talks, the more I realize how much I needed to know what has happened in Yosemite in my absence.

"Enough of me jabbering. What about you, dear Floy?" Billy says, wiping out a glass. "Back for good, I hope?"

I shake my head. "I'm lucky enough to be here through the summer."

"And what of . . . ?" He raises his eyebrows conspiratorially.

I make a point of scanning the saloon. Of course, none of the drunkards and cardplayers cares about my secrets, but it's fun to play along with Billy. The last time I'd seen him, I'd told him of my climbing dream, and it warms my heart that he's remembered. I lean across the bar and whisper, "Father is hoping to climb Half Dome with Mr. Anderson and then act as a guide himself."

Billy nods. "Go on, then."

"I hope to get there first."

His smile shows ill-kept teeth. "If there's anyone, man or girl, who could do it, it's you, Floy."

My fingers twitch as if a rope were already in their grasp.

"Floy," Cosie calls from the doorway, then waves at Billy. "The stage is ready."

Buoyed by Billy's confidence in me, I swig the rest of my milk. "Until next time, Billy."

"I'll be glad to see you," he says, waving me off. "And good luck!"

I bounce alongside Cosie to the stage. We've miles until we reach the Valley, yet it seems but a footstep away. For the three miles to Gentry's Station, where some of us will switch from the stage to mules, I speak only when spoken to and keep my hands nicely pressed together in my lap.

At Gentry's, I take a change of clothes from my bag and run into the trees to change. Without Cosie's help, removing my traveling dress is tricky, but I manage to do it without ripping any seams. I pull on the shirt and pants I traded Johnny a live scrub jay for last summer. Not my fault it flew away after one day. Tucking the dress under my arm, I stride back to the pack mules and stuff my dress away.

Grandmother considers my outfit, then nods once. Father recommends women wear loose-fitting pants that hang below the knee, known as Yosemite bloomers, when riding down the steep and treacherous trail into the Valley. Riding astride instead of sidesaddle is not only more comfortable but also safer for rider and mule. I'm only wearing what's prudent.

"Over here, Floy!"

Willie waves out the window of the stage—not the steadiest rider, he'll be safer inside with Grandmother. Cosie sits on the driver's seat, next to a tall man wearing a pinstripe vest and top hat. Widely known as one of the best stagecoach drivers in the West, George Monroe will drive our stage down the precarious trail into the Valley.

"Good day, Mr. Monroe," I say.

He tips the brim of his hat with a strong brown hand. "Nice to see you, Miss Florence."

"Your mount is tied, just there." Cosie points to a mule hitched to the back of the stage.

Mules, being nearly as stubborn as I am, are not my favorite, but they are sure-footed, and this one looks at me with alert ears and inquisitive eyes. It'll do. As I take up the reins, a rightness falls over me like a blanket of stars at midnight. I let the feeling sink in.

It feels good to be in control!

Then I give my mule a hearty kick, and it trots off toward the front of the pack line, where Father is waiting.

The trail twists gently through the woods. A hush falls over our group. The only sounds are hoof falls in the soft duff of the forest, the rumble of the stage, the snorting of the mules, and the swish of their tails. The ride feels like a pilgrimage, the route to the holiest of valleys.

After an hour or so, we round a corner and come upon Oh My! Point. It's only a rocky outcropping and by itself a dull sight, but beyond lies the sublime land of Yosemite. El Capitan rises tall and smooth on the left. Bridal Veil Fall drops delicately over the edge of a wide notch in a cliff, the water disappearing behind treetops. And in the distance, a mere bump on the horizon, waits Half Dome.

My heart skips a beat.

What grace has been set upon this land? Such contrasts and beauty, and all here for me to commune with!

Indeed, I am a pilgrim and Half Dome is my temple.

SEVEN

Our mule train is slow but there is nothing to be done—we must pick our way down to the Valley with care. Italian stoneworkers toiled twenty weeks to complete this stretch of zigzagging road, and I grip my saddle as my mule tucks its hind legs for the steep descent. Finally, our path leads us back into the shade, and the heat is easier to endure. A low oak branch snags and tugs at my bonnet, which I wear at Grandmother's insistence. She claims it protects the skin from drying out in the sun, but I'd much rather wear a broad-brimmed Stetson like Father's. Even Willie gets one.

Oh, to have been born a boy!

The sharp slope of the road eases—a sign that the Valley floor is just ahead. I press my heels into the side of my mule, passing Father at a quick walk. Then I reach back with my hand and swat the beast on its rump.

"Hee-yah!"

The mule breaks into a lope, and I step into the stirrups to steady myself. The wind pulls at my bonnet, and its ties loosen. Soon the bonnet falls from my head, but I do not care.

Mother got it for me in San Francisco.

A few strides later, the road flattens onto the Valley floor, and now we're truly off. My mount is not the speediest of animals, but I appreciate its sure-footedness. I pull the reins, this way and that, as I steer through the open pine forest, forgoing the road. The granite cliffs of El Capitan and the Cathedral Rocks pull at my attention, but my eyes remain fixed on the way in front of me. After more than a mile, both the mule and I are breathless. The river is just a bit farther! I try to urge the animal faster, but it responds by slowing to a trot.

"All right, all right," I say, giving my mule a hearty pat on the neck. "We're here."

I pull my feet from the stirrups and loosen the reins. While the mule ambles along, my fingers play with the granite rock in my pocket, the one from the cigar box. Soon the forest ends, and the trail emerges onto the meadow below El Capitan, sparsely shadowed by the branches of broad black oak trees and tall yellow pines.

The mule picks its way back onto the road. A boulder,

dotted with mortar holes for pounding acorns, rests just off the path. It marks an Indian camp, not unlike the village Sally Ann lives in farther up the Valley. It's possible she's already returned from her family's wintering grounds near Bull Creek, and I cannot wait to see her again.

Then the mighty Merced River is before us, and it's hard to say who is more thrilled, the mule or me. It heads straight for the water's edge, scaring a rainbow trout into the deeper current. The mule drinks zealously as I jump off, quickly unlace my boots, and strip to my undergarments.

Instead of dipping a toe into the cold river—and risking retreat—I charge right in and dunk, then surface, gasping for air.

"Hurrah!" I cry to granite cliffs.

Its muzzle dripping, the mule watches me struggle to pull the pants and shirt over my wet undergarments. I scratch under its thick mane. "Dear . . . beastie! Do you have a name? I shall call you Muley and hold you dear in my heart, as the one who carried me home."

The mule is unimpressed. It lowers its head for another drink.

My clothes are nearly dry by the time the rest of our party arrives, Father and Mr. Tomlinson in the lead. Father surveys the scene: me stretched out in the meadow with a blade of grass between my teeth, gazing up at the near vertical El Capitan, and the mule hitched in the trees by a drift fence. The stage pulls up next. Mr. Monroe has given

Cosie the reins for the trip across the Valley floor. She is becoming quite adept at driving a team, and her face is bright with happiness.

I dust off my pants and walk over to my mule. Grandmother, looking quite hot and miserable, peeks out of the stage window. "Goodness, Florence," she says. "Where is your bonnet?"

"It must've come off while I was riding. I didn't realize," I say, though I know exactly where it was removed from my head.

She dabs at her flushed cheeks with a handkerchief. "You know what the sun does to one's skin."

"Is there a hat I could use instead?"

"We're not opening one of the bags, with so few miles left to travel. You'd best ride off and find it, then."

"William and Cosie will keep me company," I say, taken by the idea of adventuring together as we once did. Willie climbs down from the stage and up onto the saddle in front of me. Cosie mounts a spare mule. "We'll meet you at the bridge!"

The three of us turn back and weave our way to where the Big Oak Flat Road joins the floor of the Valley. Willie again pesters Cosie with questions about school and why he isn't allowed to attend, which she addresses with her typical calm.

Then Willie shouts, "I see it!"

Ahead, my bonnet flutters in the breeze, its long ties

tangled in the branches of a deep brown tree. A manzanita tree.

Zanita.

A shiver runs down my arms.

"Do you see that, Cosie?" I say.

A few long seconds pass before her expression darkens. "Maybe you should tell Grandmother we didn't find it."

"But we did find it," Willie says. "It's right there!"

This manzanita is taller than most, and I shall have to stand on the saddle to reach the bonnet. Of course, Muley takes the opportunity to riffle around for a mouthful of grass. I teeter for a long moment, arms outstretched.

"Floy, maybe you shouldn't—"

Then Muley steps forward, and my boots slip from the smooth leather.

Drat!

Cosie gasps as I fall. At the last second my hands catch against the tree trunk, and I bungle my way to the ground, scraping all the way down. Red spots bloom on my throbbing palms, despite the smooth bark of the manzanita. I clap my hands together and savor the sensation.

Cosie crosses her arms—as if to say *I told you so*—but she is beaming. "It's like you're alive again!"

Cosie is right. In San Francisco, I *had* stopped living. Never again! I remount, tying my bonnet securely onto the saddle horn.

The mules are eager to rejoin their herd, so we make

good time trotting toward the bridge, where a crowd of riders has formed. Willie slips from the saddle and rejoins Grandmother on the stage. Father is sharing a joyous reunion with George Leidig, who owns the hotel where we'll be staying. Mr. Leidig sympathized with Father all through the court deliberations and his ultimate eviction, as did many other Valley residents.

He faces the saddle train of tourists and gestures to Father. "The infamous James Hutchings," he says with his thick German accent. "No doubt many of you are here having read and been inspired by the stories and illustrations of Yosemite he printed! A greater champion for this divine landscape there could not be."

Father loves a crowd even more than I do. He gestures behind him to a set of three towering peaks reaching for the sky like the spires of a church. "On the far side of the Cathedral Rocks, from where you have just adventured, the grandeur of Bridal Veil Fall graces the Valley. Taller than Niagara, it would seem there is no equal."

Making comparisons to Niagara Falls, and other celebrated landscapes from all over the world, is one of Father's favorite ways to impress his audiences.

"And yet to the north of where we now stand," he continues, "lies the series of vertical cascades known by natives as Cho-Lock, which we call Yosemite Falls. What a spectacle! Upon close inspection, its magnificence increases tenfold. Its power cannot be denied! The stream leaps from the precipice, to fall farther than any other fall in this Valley. To calculate, consider that the trees at the cliff edge are seventy-five feet in height. Now, imagine . . ."

Father orates with such fervor that the crowd is captured by every word. When he's finished, one of the men dismounts to shake Father's hand. One rider pushes her horse to the front. She wears a gray pressed linen hat lavishly adorned with a long plume and what appears to be a bluebird.

How absurd!

The woman rides sidesaddle. Her ankle boots—without a speck of dirt on them—peek out from the hem of her long skirts.

I glance at Cosie. "Imagine coming all this way and never dismounting your horse!"

Cosie bites back a smile. "Behave, sister!"

The woman turns her gaze to me. "You must be Hutchings's oldest child, Florence."

"My name is Floy."

She takes in my pants—and how I'm riding astride—and her mouth turns down at the corners. "So, the rumors are true."

I shift in the saddle.

Another woman presses her horse closer. Her hat bears a long plume like her companion's, only her bird is red. "Aren't you the intrigue?" she says, as if somehow offering me a compliment. "Are you as tameless as they say?"

I do not like the way they look at me, as if I'm a prize to be snatched up and put upon a plumed hat. Rumors about me have passed among the Valley tourists ever since I was three years old, but these women are not like the usual visitors. They seem set on snobbery. I yank the reins and steer away from the crowd.

As I leave, the woman says, "Tameless, indeed."

Cosie trots after me. "Floy."

When I neither stop nor turn around, she persists. "Sister, wait!"

I pull Muley to a halt, and she reaches my side. The gentle flush on her face, combined with her still-tied bonnet, ruffled dress, and unscratched hands, makes Cosie a vision of the perfect young girl.

Everything I am not.

"You mustn't let them vex you, Floy," she says.

I draw my fingers down Muley's mane. It's not so much that they bother me, as much as that they do not *understand* me. They are not like the crowd at the train station, for whom I can control the tale. If there are to be stories about me, if I am to be a tameless girl, then let the story be mine. "We're not going back, you know."

Cosie follows my eyes. "You mean to the cabin?"

"Yes." Father's cabin was near the base of Yosemite Falls, and at night we used to go to sleep to the sound of the cascade. "Leidig's is the nicest hotel. And Mrs. Leidig's mutton and pearl barley is delicious."

"But?"

"I'd give anything to stay at the cabin instead."

When Father was evicted, the commissioners of the Yosemite Grant offered up to the public leases for our cabin and Father's Hutchings Hotel—they belong to someone else now. But my childhood was spent in and out of both buildings, and not having them be ours any longer feels wrong. "I've spent so much time wanting to return," I continue, "but I didn't think through how different things would be."

Cosie reaches for my hand and taps her finger twice against mine. "We'll be together," she says. "That will be the same."

Except you are the young lady now, I want to say. And I am the "tameless" one, a fitting name despite my protests.

All I want to be is Floy.

EIGHT

The horses and mules stamp their feet across the wooden floor of Folsom Bridge as the mighty Merced passes underneath. Snow melting in the mountains has filled the various creeks coming into the Valley, with all of the water eventually joining this river. The high water rushes past in swirls of silty gray and green. Muley's head hangs lazily, but I couldn't be more awake. I'm galloping away before the last mule even steps onto the bridge.

Ahead lies the meadow where Mr. Leidig grazes his cattle and sheep, and the animals bolt at my fast approach. Standing on the lower porch of the hotel is Mrs. Leidig , a feather duster in her hand, ready to brush off the tourists upon their return from their expedition. She squints against the bright midday sun. With a hand shielding her eyes, she doesn't recognize me until I am upon her.

"Why, Florence!" she gasps as I pull up on Muley. "Welcome home, lass!"

"Thank you, Mrs. Leidig." I drop down to the ground and throw the reins over the hitching post. "I'm so glad to be back. Now, what's for dinner? I could smell whatever delightful meal you've been cooking all the way back at the El Capitan meadow!"

Mrs. Leidig scans my damp shirt and dirty trousers, and her eyes twinkle. "Well, this'll do you little good," she says, waving the duster in her hand. "You're filthy as usual, Florence. Wash up and maybe we can find you a slice of blackberry tart."

When Mrs. Leidig uses my given name, it doesn't sound like an admonishment, for she accepts me as I am. She's like Billy Hurst—except cleaner. For her, I will wash my hands without a fuss.

I follow her through the parlor and the kitchen to the washbasin in the corner. "Use soap," she says. Once my hands are clean, I wrap my arms around her, and my return to Yosemite feels ever more real.

Then she sets a plate on the table. "Come now, lass, tell me your news."

I dig into the tart and, between mouthfuls, relay the dullness of San Francisco as well as the details of Mother and Father's imminent separation. While I talk, Mrs. Leidig heats up her iron on the stove. A looming pile of freshly cleaned sheets rests next to the kitchen table.

"And then Mother left," I say, scraping up the last bite of tart. Talking to Mrs. Leidig doesn't feel like gossiping, partly due to her kind nature and also because it's no secret that Mother wasn't happy living in Yosemite. The rough living didn't suit her artistic sensibilities, and she was never able to manage all the details of running Father's hotel. With him gone much of the time, addressing the legal case against him and lecturing up and down California, the running of the hotel had fallen on Grandmother's shoulders. "I'm not sure when we'll see Mother again."

"I see," Mrs. Leidig replies. When she flicks water at the iron, it sizzles. "And how do you feel about that?"

With my return to Yosemite and my dream of climbing Half Dome occupying all my thoughts, maybe I haven't considered Mother's departure as much as I should have. She was miserable here, just as I was miserable in San Francisco. I do not blame her for not wanting to return, and yet life in the Valley will feel peculiar without her painting in the meadows. I shift in my chair. "I guess I want her to be happy."

Mrs. Leidig nods. "As she wants you to be."

My eyes are unexpectedly damp, and I change the subject. "Is Charles home?"

Charles is almost the same age as Willie. Maybe if he sees a friend upon his arrival, Willie might feel less sad about not attending school with me and Cosie.

"Check the chicken hutch," says Mrs. Leidig.

I put my plate by the wash sink and head out the door leading from the kitchen to the garden. The large hutch is empty, save for one scraggly hen. To the river, then. On my way, I pass the rest of the birds eating grubs in Mrs. Leidig's garden.

Then Mr. Leidig and his tourist party ride past on the road, headed for Black's Hotel and its stable for saddle horses. Behind them Father rides ahead of the stage to where Muley is hitched. I help Willie out and dust him off. Then I hold Grandmother's hand while she steps down. "Thank you, Florence," she says. "Was Mrs. Leidig here when you arrived?"

"She's in the kitchen, ironing."

"It's clear you've had a treat. Wipe your face."

I rub my arm across my mouth, and a purple smear of blackberry appears on my sleeve.

"Oh dear," Grandmother says. I'm about to remind her that my return to Yosemite, to this less civilized but improved version of me, was her idea, when Mrs. Leidig steps onto the porch and waves her in.

"Come on," I say to Cosie and Willie. "I think I know where Charles might be." With all this runoff, there's bound to be areas of the meadows that are flooded, and these are the best places to look for frog eggs.

We spy Charles across the meadow in the shade of a

large black oak, wading in ankle-deep water with his pants rolled up.

Willie runs ahead. "Charles!"

"That was sisterly of you," Cosie says.

"Yes, well," I say, thinking back to our meeting on the stairwell of Grandmother's boardinghouse. "If he's happy, I won't feel so bad about him staying behind."

Other silhouettes move in the shade as we approach. One of them is Johnny Boitano, whose father works as a horse packer for expeditions into the high country. His pants are rolled up like Charles's. The other is Delia Howard, daughter of Captain William Howard, who now runs the Mirror Lake House. It *is* good to see them, and I pick up my pace.

Delia spies us and skirts around the edge of the spring pool. "Cosie! Floy!"

I slow to let Cosie go first. Delia hugs Cosie, who squeals in delight.

"Delia, you look so grown-up!" Cosie says.

Delia's not much older than I am, but she's dressed like her mother. She runs her hands down the billowy sleeves of her dress. "Isn't it fancy? Father brought it from Sacramento."

"Can you hike in that?" I ask.

She shrugs. "I don't have time to hike anymore. When I'm not at school, I'll be helping my mother at Mirror Lake House."

Last summer, Delia would have preferred to spend an afternoon identifying wildflowers and collecting lichen. When she and Cosie move toward a log to share stories, I do not follow. Instead I remove my boots, roll up my pants, and wade into the cool water to the middle of the pond, where the three boys stand in a tight circle. "What are you looking at?" I ask, peering between Willie and Charles.

Johnny holds a snake with black, red, and yellow bands of color around its body. He grips it just behind its head. The snake's mouth opens, and its body begins to writhe and twist around his arm.

"You're holding it too tight," I say.

Johnny's curly brown hair falls into his eyes as he looks up. "Oh hello, Floy." He takes in my pants and shirt—his own clothes last summer.

"Hi, Johnny. Here, let me show you how to hold that thing." I reach over Willie's shoulder for the snake, but Johnny pulls his hands out of reach.

"I can do it."

I blink. Johnny always lets me hold the snakes. "Yes, but you're hurting it."

"I know how to hold a snake, Floy." He loosens his fingers at the snake's head, and its mouth closes, tongue flicking out. "See?"

Willie strokes the smooth scales of the snake, but when its tail twitches, his hand snaps back.

"It's not poisonous," Johnny and I say at the same time.

Johnny's gaze meets mine, and I hold his stare. He used to make silly faces to force a laugh out of me, but today he looks away.

The snake is twisting harder now. Charles flips over its tail. "Is that where it comes out?" he says, pointing at the tiny slit near the snake's tail.

Out squirts a vile-smelling liquid, splattering Johnny's arm. Charles shrieks and jumps back, his cheeks pinking in embarrassment.

Willie slaps his hand against his stomach and laughs. "That was disgusting!" Then he points at Johnny. "Make it do that again!"

Now I'm laughing, too. "Oh, Willie!"

"Do it again!" he repeats.

Johnny glares at me. He splashes through the water to the far side of the pool, which is thick with sedges and grasses. There he lowers his hands and lets the snake slip away into the plants. The excitement over, Delia mentions the possibility of pie in the Leidigs' kitchen, and Charles and Willie at once leave the pool.

Alone with just me, Johnny splashes water over his arm to clean it. "It's not funny, Floy."

I wipe at my eyes. "Yes, it was."

"I got snake mess all over me." He scrubs a little harder, even though there's nothing left.

I splash at him with my foot, missing by a mile, and he glares. "Quit it, Florence!"

"I've *told* you not to call me that."

I slosh away through the water. It's one thing to let go of the judgment of those snobby women, but the way Johnny is acting is making my skin itch. This day, this reunion with my home, is supposed to be glorious! I refuse to let him bother me.

"Floy, wait."

I turn to see Johnny shoving his hands into his pockets. "I am glad you're back," he says. He watches me with a hopeful expression, but I suddenly just want to be alone.

"I'll see you," I say, then pick up my shoes and start making my way back to Leidig's Hotel.

"Let's go fishing tomorrow!" Johnny calls.

I wave and keep walking.

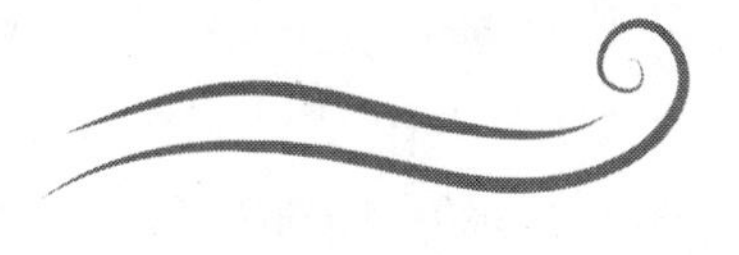

NINE

The next morning, Father is already pontificating in the parlor when I come down the stairs. Around him is a loose circle of people, some are from Mr. Leidig's tourist group and others are guests of the hotel. Grandmother sits in a high-backed chair with a groggy Willie pressed against her side. I step inside quietly and lean against the wall to listen while Father speaks.

"You ask about the origin of Yosemite," he says, stroking his beard. "Rigorous is the debate. God's great creation, this world we live in, is ever changing. A river's path might move and shift. Rocks fall from high up these granite cliffs with regularity."

"Why, Mr. Leidig showed us a collection of large boulders on our tour yesterday," a man says. "Claimed they fell during a fierce shaking of the earth a few years back."

"Indeed, large boulders fell during an earthquake not four years ago," Father says, his eyes starting to twinkle. "There are some people who believe an enormous block of land dropped in a single stroke of a quake, creating the deep cañon we stand in today."

Heads nod as he talks. Father was always a better orator than hotel owner—but I've heard it all before. I press my hands into my stomach to keep it from growling.

Surveying his rapt crowd, Father presses down the front of his jacket and continues. "Still others look to a great and violent shaking of the earth as having caused this Valley to split apart. Even Mr. Josiah Whitney, formerly of the California Geological Survey, ascribed to the belief in a cataclysmic creation of Yosemite. Neither of those theories is correct. Instead—"

"A great glacier of ice filled this Valley and covered the mountains beyond," I say, pushing off the wall. Father settles into an open chair and motions for me to continue. "The weight of the ice scraped and pressed against the rock, grinding it bit by bit and carrying it away with meltwater."

The woman who yesterday called me *tameless* speaks up. "And where, child, has all that ice gone?"

"Why, it melted!"

A few guests chuckle.

"Florence," Father says. He is guiding me, as he often does. I imagine what he might say to persuade a skeptic. "Just yesterday," I say as though I'm the teacher, the woman my student, "did you not witness the narrow hanging cañon of Bridal Veil Fall? A small glacier carved out that cañon before joining the one moving through Yosemite Valley. Or the moraine of jumbled rocks left by the glacier at the foot of El Capitan? Those rocks belong not to the cliffs of the Valley but to high peaks ten miles or more away!"

My entire body pulses with energy. Listening to Father's speeches may have become a touch weary to me, but I love giving them as much as he does.

"Mr. Leidig may have mentioned some of those things," the woman says.

Why does she remain unconvinced?

Then her eyes flit to my legs—or rather to the dress Grandmother insists I wear to school, and I know.

To her, I am just an eleven-year-old girl, and I should neither know nor speak of such things. I wish it weren't so hard for her to believe I have something to contribute. Cosie and I grew up listening to Father exchange ideas with all manner of scientists, artists, and philosophers. In fact, Father has always encouraged us to engage in their great debates. There is not an ounce of Yosemite's history I do not know. No trail I have not climbed—except Half Dome, of course. But she knows none of this. I take a deep breath and start again. "Mr. Muir, in an article for the *Overland Monthly*, clearly describes Yosemite's glaciers and their origins. I cannot recommend it enough."

The woman sighs impatiently and looks to Father.

"My daughter is correct," he says, standing. "In fact, I've a copy of the article should anyone care to read it."

She motions for him to continue. As Father launches further into the evidence for Yosemite's glacial history, I sink back against the wall.

Then Cosie steps into the parlor, and all eyes look to her.

"Good morning," she says. "I'm sorry for the interruption, but Floy and I must ready for school."

The woman offers me a satisfied smile. It's time for the child to return to the activities proper young ladies should engage in.

Man alive! She's the one with the absurd hat!

I push past Cosie into the dining room. Mrs. Leidig already has two plates of ham and eggs set out for us. I throw myself into the chair and begin eating, barely looking up as Mrs. Leidig brings me a fresh glass of milk.

"Thank you," Cosie says, sitting down across from me.

"You're welcome, dear," replies Mrs. Leidig.

I keep eating. She lingers by the table before returning to the kitchen.

"Floy." Cosie nudges me. "It's Mrs. Leidig."

Taking a long swallow of milk, I study my sister. She always knows how to act and how to speak properly to people. Am I always to be reminded of our differences? My heart withers a little. It's not Cosie I'm mad at. She cannot be anything but herself, just as I cannot be anything save me. Has that become unacceptable? Or at least more unacceptable than usual?

"Why wouldn't that woman listen to me?"

Cosie shrugs and takes a bite of ham. "I haven't read Mr. Muir's articles. Should I?"

"I suppose," I say, and set my unfinished breakfast aside. "Meet me by the river at our spot. Ten minutes."

"All right."

I carry my plate to the kitchen. Mrs. Leidig looks up from cutting onions and brushes a hand against her eye.

"Thank you for breakfast, Mrs. Leidig. Ham is my favorite."

"Oh, child," she says. "You are most welcome." She wipes at her eye again.

"Could I help you? Onions never bother me." This couldn't be farther from the truth—my eyes are beginning to water even from across the room!

"Aren't you a dear? You'd best be off to school." She beckons me with her hand. I slip under her arm for a quick hug, relieved to have set things right.

Out in the cool morning air, I walk through the sparse community of Yosemite Village. Steam already billows from Flores' Laundry, and a line of saddle horses stands outside Black's Hotel and Livery. Guests linger on the porch, awaiting the day's expedition. A cloud of dark smoke chokes the doorway to Mr. Anderson's blacksmith forge. Might the Scotsman be working on new iron bolts for Half Dome? I march past without looking up. Once at the edge of the Merced River, I follow it upstream to where a series of channels come together. There I sit in the grass and wait for Cosie.

Half Dome is obscured from this spot, so I settle for studying the swirling water and the meadow beyond. Even in the early-morning light, the fresh green of the sedges is brilliant. Blackbirds flash red wing patches as they fly from willow to willow, and a trout rises in the river. I try to imagine being a fish or a bird or even a mosquito, living without a care for what people might think of them. Then again, what glorious views this Valley offers, and certainly the blackbirds cannot appreciate the place as I do.

To dream of Half Dome is a human preoccupation, and one I would not trade for anything.

Even if I have to deal with women wearing absurd hats.

On the other side of the river, someone walks down the fishing path. It's a girl, with brown skin and straight black hair that is cropped at her shoulder and again across her forehead.

"Sally Ann!" I call out, but she cannot hear me over the roar of the Merced. I pick up a handful of rocks and toss one into the river ahead of Sally Ann's view. She looks up, and I wave.

She lifts her hand. "Hello!"

"Welcome back," I shout over the rushing water.

"You look taller," she calls back. She points to my dress.

A plain shift I wore last year, it now rests a smidge too high above my boots. I'd hoped no one would notice, but little gets past Sally Ann.

There's no time to trade stories. The river gushes between us, and Cosie will soon arrive for the walk to school. Our classroom is located on the sunny north side of the Valley, near Sally Ann's village, but Sally Ann will not be in attendance. When Father campaigned for a school, he did not include the Indian children in the plans.

Where is Sally Ann headed now?

I toss another rock into the river near her feet. Water splashes up, and she jumps back, laughing. "See you soon!" Then she waves once more before striking off down the river.

Smiling, I lean back into the prickly grass and wait for Cosie.

TEN

To avoid getting our feet wet in the flooded meadow, Cosie and I walk along the boardwalk owned by the Cosmopolitan Saloon. The elevated wooden slats stop not far from Father's former hotel, located just across from the Cosmopolitan and now under new proprietorship. The closer we get, the faster my heart beats. Like at Black's Hotel, a group of tourists is mounting up for the day's excursions. Instead of heading off on my own adventure, I'm stuck going to school.

May the mules piss on their riders' shoes!

I duck my head and hurry past. Even Cosie picks up her pace.

Once over the Merced River, via the second bridge Father

built on this spot, we chance upon a group of Indian men with strings of rainbow trout dangling off their shoulders. Cosie waves to a tall man with a mustache. It's Tom, a Paiute who has worked for Father since I was quite young. Not only does he deliver the Valley's letters, but he's also been helping Father with a new business, selling the seeds of California plants to buyers all around the world.

He offers me a nod as I approach. "You are back then, all of you?"

"Father is in the parlor at Leidig's. Hey! That's some catch, Louie," I say, pointing to the load of rainbows carried by one of the other men.

"Fish are hungry in the spring," Louie replies.

The trout in Yosemite's rivers are notoriously difficult to catch, and the men will sell their haul to tourists for twenty-five cents a bunch. Cosie and I wave goodbye and continue through the sparse pines toward Indian Cañon. School will take place on the sunny side of the Valley, between Father's old cabin and the Indian village. Mr. Chestnutwood, who taught us last summer, has already abandoned us for a school near Stockton. He will not be missed. In his stead, Ida Howard, Delia's fourteen-year-old sister, will teach our ragtag crew.

We find Ida by the edge of Indian Creek. She is arranging wooden boxes into the makeshift circle that will serve as our classroom. Delia, with her four younger siblings in tow, arrives just after Cosie and I do. There are a few more familiar faces, along with some new ones. The opening of the stage roads has meant more tourists, and with them more families have moved to the Valley to serve them.

Delia approaches, dragging her youngest brother, Royal, by the hand. Today, her dress is plain with short sleeves and a low waist. It's a practical choice that mirrors my own.

"Hi, Delia," I say.

"Hello, Floy," she replies. "I hope we don't have to sit here too long. The day is going to be boiling. Can't you feel it?" She dabs at her neck with a handkerchief just as Grandmother does. I resist rolling my eyes. Turns out that even without a woman's dress, Delia seems to have forgotten she is only twelve.

Cosie picks the box next to Delia's. "Sit with us."

I glance at Johnny, sharing a cedar log with Charles, the only Leidig child old enough to attend. Johnny waves as if I hadn't shunned him yesterday.

"Floy?" Cosie touches my hand.

In my hesitation, Delia's younger sister Carrie plops down in the place next to Cosie, sparing me the discomfort of rejecting my sister and Delia.

"Tomorrow," I promise, and then I make my way to Johnny's log and settle myself between him and Charles.

Drat!

If Charles is here, then Willie will be left to look after

the younger Leidig children. There is little I can do to help him now, but maybe I can find him a lizard on the way home to cheer him up.

"Hey, Charles," I say. "Did you get any snake mess in your eye?"

He wrinkles his nose. "Didn't know that would happen."

"You asked for it!"

On my other side, Johnny grunts.

"You asked for it, too," I say.

Johnny shakes his head. "Maybe you shouldn't tease so much."

"Since when is teasing not allowed?" I try to poke him in the side, but he scoots away.

"Delia doesn't tease," he says. "Neither does your sister."

I wince.

He takes in my wounded expression. "I don't mean anything by it, Floy. It's only, girls shouldn't tease."

"Stop telling me what to do," I say lamely. "I'm moving."

The log and all the crates are taken, and the only free place in the circle is at the base of a large oak. It's perfect. Kicking some sticks out of the way, I make a seat on the ground and lean back against the tree. The canopy is full of fresh green leaves, and a breeze shakes the highest branches. If I can't talk to my friends, then at least I'll have something better to look at than the walls of Mrs. Pinkerton's classroom.

Ida starts us off with a rigorous lesson in mathematics. "What is ninety-seven minus forty-eight?" she asks. There are no slates or chalk with which to write like we had in the city, so we must do the calculations in our heads.

Albert Howard raises his hand. "Forty-one!"

Ida smiles encouragingly at her brother. "Try again, Albie."

He scrunches up his face. "Fifty-one?"

"Oh, Albert, quit guessing," I say. "The answer is forty-nine."

"Fifty-nine," Johnny counters.

"Forty-nine."

Ida's smile disappears. "Florence, Johnny, don't call out."

"Yes, Miss Howard," Johnny says.

Ida raises her eyebrows at me, as if to say *See how polite Johnny is?* She's barely two years older than I am. But make her teacher and now she expects to be called Miss? Just last summer she was a student herself! I'm about to say as much when I see Cosie's face. The withering glance she gives me is too reminiscent of Father. I can almost hear her pleading.

"Have a care, Florence," Father said as we prepared for the journey. "I know what it means to you, this return to Yosemite. You must hold to my expectations and those of your grandmother."

The implication was clear.

If I do not behave, I will be sent back to the Pine Street boardinghouse.

When Ida gives the answer—forty-nine, just as I had calculated—I say nothing. For the rest of the math lesson, I answer only when called on. During elocution, Ida requires each one of us to stand in front of the group and recite the poem of our choosing. When it's my turn, I brush the leaves from my dress, close my eyes, and speak my favorite lines from *Alice's Adventures in Wonderland*. I'm nearly finished when Johnny throws a pine cone at me. It bounces off me and onto the ground. I snatch a second cone in midair and toss it back. The cone hits him squarely on the ear, and he claps his hand over the side of his head.

"Florence," Ida snaps.

I lift my eyebrows, as she did, and point to Johnny.

"Just sit down," she says wearily.

Johnny smirks. I stick my tongue out at him and slump down at the base of my tree.

Halfway through our spelling lesson, which Ida delivers by writing out words onto the slats of a wooden crate, Royal falls asleep on Delia's shoulder. Ida gently taps her stick against the crate to wake him up.

She surveys the group. "It's hot. Let's take a break for lunch."

Cosie and I wander through the pines with Delia toward Indian Creek. Johnny trails behind.

"I want to go exploring," I say, cupping my hands in the creek and watching the water stream over them. "Remember when we hiked to the spring near the mouth of Tenaya Cañon?"

Cosie dips our shared cup, drinks, and then passes the cup to Delia.

"I twisted my ankle," Delia says between sips. "No, thank you."

"I'd never let a twisted ankle stop me. And you used to enjoy a good adventure. Let's go!"

"We've only just arrived," Cosie laments.

"Yes, and so far all we've done is elocution."

"I'm glad to be in school."

"Well, I didn't come back to Yosemite to learn how to spell *courageous."*

She looks to the east, and I know she's thinking about Half Dome. Will she mention my secret? Delia might tell her parents, who would certainly tell Father. I hold my breath.

"Miss Howard's actually a good teacher," Cosie says finally.

Delia snorts. "No, she isn't. She's just copying what Mr. Chestnutwood did."

"Cosie's right," I say. "Ida's doing a decent job. You never had Mrs. Pinkerton—she could bore the legs off a table!"

Johnny laughs.

"What about you, Johnny?" I say. "Want to scramble to the base of Yosemite Falls?"

He tosses a rock into the stream. "I guess I could go."

I clap my hands. "We can leave after Ida's done with us."

Johnny shakes his head. "I can't today. An expedition is returning from the high country, and I have to help my dad with the horses."

"Tomorrow, then." I throw my head back and yip like a coyote.

As we walk back to Ida's makeshift classroom, Cosie links her arm in mine. "I don't want to leave," she says.

"Don't fret! School will happen again tomorrow, and the next day, and the next."

She bumps her shoulder against mine. "I'm not talking about school, though I think I do want to be a teacher someday."

I raise an eyebrow.

She shrugs. "I was trying to say that I want to be here—in Yosemite—just as much as you do."

I turn my attention to the leaves fluttering in the warm breeze. "Did you see that Charles was here? Willie must be so upset to be all alone. I'm bringing him a lizard to cheer him up."

"Are you even listening?"

I squeeze her arm. "I am. And I know what you're worried about. I promise to do my best."

The weight of her reminder drops upon me like a heavy fur coat in summer. If I cannot abide Father's expectations, I am to be sent back to San Francisco.

And Cosie and Willie will go with me.

I tug my sister forward. "Come on. Let's count the ways you'd be an even better teacher than Ida."

ELEVEN

The next day, Johnny does not show up for school. After I say my goodbyes to Ida, Cosie, and Delia, I run back to Yosemite Village, change into my pants, and set off to search for Johnny. I find him in the main corral, tightening up the cinch on a pack mule. He nudges the mule's belly with his knee. The animal releases a breath of air, and Johnny pulls the cinch tighter.

I step up onto the bottom rail of the fence and lean over. "Where were you today?"

He pulls on the pack saddle, testing the tightness of the rigging, then he dusts off his hands and approaches the fence. "One of the stable hands got bucked off this wild mare and broke his collarbone. I'm stuck here for a while."

It's not his fault, but I duck my head and pull a piece of

hay from the fence so he can't see my disappointment. "I guess I should be off, then."

"Maybe tomorrow?"

"Sure." I offer him a weak smile. "Tomorrow."

He sends me off with a piece of salted pork left over from his lunch, and I head west toward Yosemite Falls. With the clouds covering the sky, it's not much warmer than springtime in San Francisco. Still, moving through the forest on my first adventure since returning to the Valley makes the blood rush through my limbs.

I jog along a fishing trail until I find a good place to cross the Merced. Then I teeter over on a thin log, my arms outstretched, and arrive at the edge of a broad meadow. Water floods through the grass and sedge, just as in the meadow near Leidig's. Since today I'm not looking for toads or snakes, I skirt the inundated area in search of drier ground.

I arrive at Father's old cabin. Our former home looks much the same. The shingled roof looks no worse the wear after the winter, and the elderberry bushes that Mother planted have fully leafed out.

My childhood here was glorious! I toddled through the forest, turning over logs and collecting feathers I'd found on the ground, always with a lizard or a wasp tucked away in my pocket. I had no chores or responsibilities. And in the summer, there were always new people visiting the Valley—new people to entertain me. Mr. Muybridge, the photographer, taught me how to smoke a corncob pipe.

It wasn't long after that Mrs. Yelverton came to stay at Father's hotel on the other side of the Valley. That visit didn't turn out so well for me.

She wrote *Zanita* shortly afterward.

I pause in front of the door. It's ajar, as if the new lease owner couldn't be bothered to close it, but I do not enter. There is no smoke billowing from the chimney, no cheery curtains in the windows, and no inviting, handmade chairs to welcome a weary adventurer home.

I can't stand the sight of it.

I leave the cabin behind and don't even offer the orchard or strawberry patch a second glance. Instead, I wonder among the pines along one of Yosemite Creek's many channels until I reach Father's old sawmill. It's been out of use longer than the cabin and brings up fewer memories. I scramble up the rickety ladder inside to a small room built out over one edge of the mill. Mr. Muir designed it for himself when he worked for Father, and on occasion he invited Cosie, Willie, and me to hear the creek water trickling underneath. I lie on my back and look up through the hole Mr. Muir cut in the roof. My eyes fall right upon Half Dome.

Man alive! It never fails to steal my breath!

I study the western slope of Half Dome—or Tissiack as Sally Ann calls it. Is the eastern side, where Mr. Anderson climbed, as sheer? I visualize myself moving up a tawny streak in the rock, reaching for imaginary knobs to hold on to. In my daydream, a chittering swallow zips past, and the wind sends wisps of hair snapping at my cheeks. My arms ache from the strain of the climb, but I persevere until the rock begins to level out. Once atop the summit, I start anew, this time taking a different pretend route. Beneath me, through the slatted floor of Mr. Muir's hang nest, the creek babbles. The sound lulls me into dreaming. Only then do I notice the deep hum blending with the burble of the water.

I bolt upright, almost hitting myself on a low shelf built into the wall. In an instant, I'm stumbling down the ladder and out the door.

Years ago, Father hand-dug a trench to send water to the mill, and I trail it all the way to where Yosemite Creek first starts to spread out. The hum quickly grows into an even deeper rumble. A final turn around a boulder and the forest opens onto the main creek. I take in the scene from the safety of the trees. The water is a torrent, rising and falling in white waves. There is no way to cross—and no need to. All it takes is a single step beyond the trees and onto a flat rock, and I am drenched in the blowing spray. Lower Yosemite Fall must be over one hundred feet away, but I'm as good as in it!

I spread my arms wide and tip my head back, savoring the chilly water against my skin. The roar of the falls is deafening, but I do not care.

This! This is why I ran away from school!

To experience the power of Yosemite!

TWELVE

Late spring burns into early summer. The snow in the high country continues to melt in the warmth, and the streambeds remain flooded by the runoff. Yosemite Falls thunder even louder—I can hear it from a mile away. The meadow grasses struggle to reach their highest, only to be chewed down by the horses, sheep, and cattle dotting the Valley floor. Even the tiniest scrap of shade swarms with mosquitoes.

My weeks are filled with lessons with Ida, collecting eggs for Mrs. Leidig, running odd errands for Grandmother, and, of course, enduring Father's parlor talks. If I am lucky, there is time each day for an afternoon scramble up the rocks of a talus slope or to fish by the river, though none of these outings could count as a true adventure.

One morning in late June, I am washing mud from Willie's hands while catching glimpses of the sunlight hitting the treetops. "There. Now shake them—No!" I bite back a laugh. "Don't wipe them on your dirty pants!"

He pulls his hands out of mine and tries to escape back to the chicken hutch. I manage to grab his shoulders and haul him back to the washbasin. "Let's get this over with. Then I can go to school and you can play with John Henry."

"He's only two. He's boring. Spending all day in this hotel is boring." He looks up at me. "Florence, won't you stay with me?"

I release his hands and step back from the basin. Hadn't Willie said nearly the same words to me at Grandmother's boardinghouse, not two months ago? Returning to Yosemite almost let me forget that I'd been about to run away, run back to this place. I'd gotten what I wanted without having to lift a finger. Well, most of what I wanted.

Willie tugs on my apron. "Please, Sister, stay. *You're* not boring."

I touch his cheek. "Oh, Willie."

"I'll go anywhere. Just take me with you."

Given a day without school or obligations, a full day from sunrise to sunset, there are so many things we could do, like hike to the bottom of Ribbon Fall or walk the length of El Capitan's base. I could carry Willie part of the way, or perhaps we could convince Mrs. Leidig to lend us a mule.

I don't want to do any of those things.

I want to see Half Dome.

Up close.

And that means, no Willie.

A plan solidifies as if it's been waiting all this time. Maybe it has. I squat down and take in his pleading eyes. A lizard will not suffice this time. "I am sorry, Willie. Today won't work. Are you free on Saturday? I know the way to a patch of wild strawberries."

After a long hug, I send him out the door, making sure he has an extra piece of tart in his pocket and a promise to let him eat most of the wild berries we find. He trots off in his lopsided way and disappears around the corner of the hotel.

I sit down on the step to clear my thoughts. Why does Willie always make my chest hurt? I *will* make it up to him, but today I must pick up the pieces of my forgotten dream.

I brush off my apron and sneak into the kitchen. A slice of mutton pie wrapped in muslin and one of the apples Mrs. Leidig stored over the winter go into my satchel along with a canteen of water, which I plan to refill from Tenaya Creek. This is far more than the tea and crackers Mr. Muir used to take into the high country, so I figure it'll do me just fine for the two days I plan to be gone.

Done in the kitchen, I sneak up the stairs to hide a note

in Cosie's hairbrush. It tells her not to worry. She likely won't find the note until tonight, meaning no one can stop me before I'm well on my way to the summit. Then, as the linen partitions between our rooms are far from soundproof, I change clothes as quietly as I can.

I can't very well climb Half Dome in a dress!

THIRTEEN

In an hour, the eastern edge of Yosemite Village is well behind me. Instead of taking the road to Mirror Lake, where I could be spotted by Captain Howard or a tourist wagon from his Mirror Lake House, I pass unnoticed in the trees. My legs move quickly over the uneven ground, but my stomach is buzzing and I can feel the blood pulsing through my fingers. Will this be as easy as in my imaginings? As the distance from Yosemite Village increases, my pace—and my thoughts—slow.

A twig snaps. I spin around but see nothing unusual. Might be a bear. I sniff the air for musk. Smelling nothing but cedar trees, I find a moss-covered rock and sit. Johnny steps into view, wearing a sheepish look on his face.

"Are you following me?" I ask. For all the begging I've

done to get people to accompany me on outings, it's likely not the welcome he's expecting.

"Where're you off to?" he says.

I hesitate. If I tell him, it's possible he might tell my grandmother. "Nowhere. Shouldn't you be in school?"

"Shouldn't you?" He sits on a rock opposite me and rubs his outstretched legs. He looks past me. "Where are you going, anyway? Tenaya Cañon?"

I shake my head. "Not telling."

"Come on." His shoulders sag. "I just . . . you used to tell me everything."

"And you used to treat me like I wasn't a girl."

"But you *are* a girl."

"I'm Floy."

I stare into my hands. Not only is talking with Johnny wasting daylight, it's making me feel all twisted up inside. Maybe I *should* let him come. It could be like before, except bigger and better. The words spill out before I can second-guess myself. "I am climbing Half Dome."

His brows pinch together. "You're going the wrong way."

"If I take the ladders past Vernal Fall or the horse trail up to Snow's hotel, then someone will surely see me. Even this way, I have to avoid the road to Mirror Lake House." I hold his gaze so he will understand what I'm not saying—that I do not want Father to find out.

At least not until I've gained the summit and made it back home, victorious.

"There's no path the way you're going," Johnny says.

I'm beginning to regret telling him, because I can guess what he will say next—that the way is too dangerous without a trail. But I've no space in my mind for warnings or doubts. "I can do it."

He shakes his head. "Don't, Floy."

When I start walking, he leaps up to follow.

"I told you not to think about coming with me," I say.

"I'm not stupid enough to try something like that."

"Then why are you following me?"

He flings up his hands. "To stop you, that's why!"

He doesn't retreat, so I quicken my pace despite the fallen logs and lichen-covered rocks. Johnny matches my speed, breathing hard, but keeps his distance. Then the forest opens onto a boulder field, and I scramble higher and faster, widening the space between us. When I glance over my shoulder, I see the broad mirrored surface of Mirror Lake below. The lake rests at the base of Half Dome, and I chance a look.

A rocky slab rises from the boulder field. Trees cling improbably to rounded ledges that lead up to a vertical face. The most obvious crack extending up the ledges will be my route. Once at the bottom of Half Dome's sheer face, I can skirt the base to the east and connect with the shoulder where George Anderson's infamous iron eyebolts and knotted rope await me.

Man alive! It's as if I am already there!

"Floy, wait!"

I do not stop.

I cannot.

My fingers grasp desperately for holds while I press my boots onto grainy lips of rock. Higher and higher I climb. Johnny disappears below a bulge, and eventually he stops calling for me. He's gone.

I stop and rest. My hands shake from the exertion, and my throat is parched. After draining my canteen, I start on my apple, chewing every bit of skin and then flicking the stem over the bulge. I wipe my hands on my pants and survey the ledge. It's wide enough for a few horses to stand on, but there is no obvious way to reach the next one, more than twenty feet above me. Reaching as high as I can, I take hold of a nub of rock and pull. The rock breaks off in my hand, and I fall back onto the ledge.

Why didn't I think to bring a rope?

Hours pass as I try to puzzle a way up. Each attempt results in only a few more inches gained. Finally, my arms are spent, and climbing back down to the ledge is my only option. All that effort and I am no closer to my goal! It's clear that I will have to return later with more supplies. I try to retreat over the bulge, but I cannot see the footholds.

I am stuck.

I slide down to sit against the rock. The sun is now an orange orb on the horizon, and soon darkness will be upon me. My food is long gone, and all that remains in my satchel is the empty canteen and the granite rock from my cigar box, which brings me no joy now. It's all I can do to keep my eyes open. I rub my dry throat and wrap my arms around my shaking body.

"It's your own fault, Floy Hutchings," I say to myself. In my mind, I've always scaled Half Dome on my own. It's what I've wanted, above all. Now the cold night feels like too much to bear alone.

The rock feels sharp against my back, and I fidget to get comfortable. None of my previous adventures ever left me in such a predicament. Still, why hadn't I let Cosie know where I was headed? How will anyone find me? A bat swoops low over my head, and I flinch.

Then a light at Mirror Lake House begins to twinkle in the twilight—it's closer than I expected. I swallow my disappointment, but its nearness is my only hope.

"Help!" I call out. "Help! Someone! Captain Howard, anyone!"

I shout until I can shout no more. Cosie was right. The climb is too dangerous. Or maybe I am too young. Or just a girl. I tuck my head against my knees and cry.

FOURTEEN

Moonlight is starting to hit the cliffs across the Valley, but illumination does little to ease my suffering. My back and legs are sore from this rocky perch, and seeing my surroundings better only confirms the hopelessness of my situation. I am pulling the collar of my shirt up around my neck just as something pings against the cliff below.

"Hello?" My voice cracks.

Another ping. I hear strained breaths and the brush of clothing against rock. Someone is climbing up.

Then a head peers over the bulge. Black hair shields a round face.

"Sally Ann?"

She pulls herself over the crest of the bulge and brushes her hands off against her plain cotton dress. "It is late," she says.

I let loose a strained laugh. "Blazes, Sally Ann! That's all you have to say?" I, for one, have never been happier to see anyone in my life.

Her eyes survey the ledge and then the crack I'd intended to follow. Will she tease me for not being able to make it? Finally, she says, "Are you all right?"

I ignore the flush of shame on my cheeks and join her at the lip of the bulge. "I'm fine. I just got stuck." Even in the dim light, my head spins from the steep drop below us. "How will we get down?"

She pulls something from around her waist. It's a thin rope twisted from Indian hemp. She passes me the end. "You can go first."

I wrap the rope round my waist and tie a knot. My fingers shake, from both exhaustion and fear. Thankfully I've followed Father across snowfields before, with ropes linking us together. When I tug on the loose end of rope, my knot holds. Sally Ann has positioned herself at the edge and motions for me to start climbing down.

I have no choice. I stretch my legs out over the bulge and inch my body down after them. Sally Ann keeps the rope taut, providing just enough assurance that I will be able to descend the ten feet to the lower ledge without slipping. When she follows, I use my hands to guide her feet toward the best places to step.

Once she is down, I ask, "How did you find me?"

She takes her end of the rope and fixes it around her waist. "I was getting water for Mrs. Howard when I heard you calling."

What a stroke of luck! Sally Ann and her brothers sometimes fetch water for the hotels, and the Mirror Lake House provides refreshments and meals to tourists who venture up to the lake. I touch my tender throat.

"I stopped calling so long ago."

She checks her knot. "I went back for a rope."

For the next ledge, she climbs down first. We descend in turns, while barely speaking. I had made it far enough to escape from Johnny—and had scarcely left the safety of the boulder field. Without Sally Ann, I'd still be partway up the slabs, with a chilly night ahead of me. I shiver at the thought. Then it hits me. Had Johnny made it down safely? Even though I know he had the advantage of daylight, a seed of worry grows in my mind.

By the time we reach the bottom, it is truly dark. We stumble over the rocks and logs until the clear path of the wagon road opens up before us. Our pace quickens.

"Thank you," I say, breaking the silence. The words seem too small for how I feel.

"You're welcome."

"I had not planned on sleeping up there," I offer.

"Too cold at night."

I rub my shoulder, still sore from all that time on the ledge. "How did you know I was there?"

"I saw you and Johnny walking toward Tissiack. Then only Johnny came back."

I sigh in relief. He'd made it to Mirror Lake House, at least. "Well, thank you."

She flicks me on the arm. "You said that already. And friends help each other. You helped me."

I search my memories of last summer. "I remember when there was a snake under your umacha."

She flinches. "I do not like snakes."

"Didn't we cut the rattles off?" After I'd pulled the snake out from under her family's cedar-bark house, her older brother had whacked the creature on the head with a large flat rock and smoked the oily meat over a fire. The rattles had been given to one of the toddling children in the village. "There aren't as many rattlesnakes in the Valley as there used to be."

"Many things have changed," she says.

I try to make out Sally Ann's face, but the road is enclosed by trees, and it's too dark to see her expression. "I wish it could go back to the way it was."

She pauses at the edge of Mr. Lamon's apple orchard, and I think maybe she's going to say something. Instead, she abruptly spins around and heads back along the Mirror Lake road.

"Wait, Sally Ann!"

She makes it a few feet before she turns to face me again.

"Good night, Floy."

"Good night."

I wait until her silhouette melts into the shadows and then head through the orchard for Lamon's cabin. It's been abandoned since he died last year, but the apple trees he planted are flowering even without his care. Having played here for as long as I can remember, I have no difficulty weaving through the well-spaced trees.

I glance over my shoulder in the direction Sally Ann went. If it weren't for her, I would still be up there. A shudder runs down my arm. Then a deer jumps across the faint path, startling me back into the present.

At the orchard's edge, the path rejoins the road, and I've not taken five steps when a wagon approaches. A lantern lights up the face of Johnny's father.

"Why, Florence!" he says, visibly relieved. "There you are!"

"Good evening, Mr. Boitano."

He pats the seat next to him. I climb up, and a weariness settles over my body. "I'm terribly sorry. Are you out here just for me?"

He clucks to his team. "Your grandmother's quite upset. No one knew where you'd went."

"Did Johnny . . ." I can't finish the question.

"At first we thought you were together, but he claimed he'd been hanging out in the stable with the new filly."

Oh, Johnny! He made it up and down the talus, all trying to help me. It's all I can do to stay upright. I'd hoped to return victorious, but now, even in spite of the note I left for Cosie, people are in distress over me. And what if Grandmother sends us back because of my selfishness?

"Could we go a little faster?" I say, suddenly eager to be done with this horrid day, no matter the punishment that awaits me.

Mr. Boitano flicks the reins, and we're soon passing through Yosemite Village. "Good night, Florence," he says as we pull up at Leidig's Hotel. "I'm glad you're all right."

"Thank you, Mr. Boitano," I say. "And tell Johnny I'm back, will you?"

Nothing good lies in store for me inside. In my haste for adventure, I'd only thought of what a successful climb of Half Dome would bring. I hadn't considered what might happen if I failed. Truly, I'm lucky to be alive.

I find Grandmother in the parlor and nearly stumble as her arms fly around me. "Oh, Florence!"

I swallow an unexpected sob and return her embrace. She pushes me into a chair and looks down her nose at me. "I am furious." She presses her lips together. "But I am also quite glad you are safe."

Mrs. Leidig steps into the room and lifts a hand to her bosom as she sees me. "Oh, goodness, what a relief. I'll send George out to look for James."

After Mrs. Leidig is gone, I say, "Father's looking for me?"

"Of course," Grandmother says. "You left, Florence. *Again.*"

"I was planning to return," I say shakily. "And I didn't go far." She needn't know too much more about my misadventure.

"You cannot wander off by yourself."

"Why not?"

The question is an honest one. I'm not being impertinent. Today is proof enough that she is right, but I don't understand why everything is changing so.

"You're not a little girl anymore, Florence. You should know that you could have been hurt."

If I'm not a little girl, why can't I be trusted?

Grandmother brushes her hand against my cheek, and I'm distracted by the unexpected tenderness in her touch and by how nice it feels. She offers me a rueful smile.

"Florence, dear. You are capable of so much more now. It's time to be responsible. It's time to grow up."

FIFTEEN

I know you're not sleeping," Cosie whispers. The morning air is brisk, and she snuggles closer to me under our thin blanket. She was asleep when I climbed into our bed last night. "I'm not mad, but I wish you'd told me where you'd gone."

"I should have." I turn my face against her shoulder. "At least Father said we're not leaving."

Grandmother and I did not wait long for Mr. Leidig to return with Father. After offering me more than a few scolding words, Father raised the likelihood of a return to San Francisco. Grandmother again—saved me from my own self. She has insisted on staying for the celebration the Howards are planning for the centennial, the one hundredth birthday of our nation. Her refusal to return to San Francisco leaves only Father to accompany us back, but surely Half Dome growing back its missing portion is more likely than that.

For the next week, instead of attending school, I will accompany Grandmother to the Mirror Lake House and help with the preparations for the Howards' party. Which is worse? Leaving Yosemite or working under the shadow of Half Dome and my failure? I pull the blanket over my head.

Cosie nudges me, and I uncover my face. "Actually, I am mad," she says.

"But we're not leaving. It's going to be all right."

She bolts up, the blanket settling against her legs. "Why, I was . . ." Then her shoulders droop, and she lies back down. "It got so dark, and I was scared."

I reach for her hand and tap her finger with mine. "I didn't mean to scare you."

"Your note was unclear—you could've gone anywhere."

Tears well in my eyes as I imagine how I would feel if she'd been the one missing. "I truly am sorry."

She tugs on my hand. "Now that I think about it," she says, "I have an idea of where you went. Just please, will you tell me next time?"

"Yes," I say, blinking tears away.

After a quick breakfast, Grandmother and I secure a ride to the Mirror Lake House with Mr. Boitano. He's delivering extra food as well as special decorations that Mrs. Howard ordered all the way from Sacramento. As we follow the road to Mirror Lake, I am forced to relive every moment. The snapped twig alerting me to Johnny's presence. His pursuit of me through the dense trees. The rocky slabs and my rescue by Sally Ann. The memories bring a special kind of punishment and are just the thing Grandmother might use to ensure that a lesson has sunk in.

Is this what growing up means?

From the buckboard of the wagon I pump my legs, wondering how hard I can swing before I fall back into Mrs. Howard's beef delivery or before the momentum sends me into the dirt. It's a good enough distraction that I almost fail to notice Sally Ann walking along a footpath toward Mirror Lake House. Her form flashes in and out of view as trees obscure the path. I call her name, but she shows no sign of having heard.

"Who are you talking to, Florence?" asks Grandmother from her spot on the spring seat.

"Sally Ann."

"I have not seen much of her this summer. How is she?"

"When she's not helping her mother, she's been working at the hotels."

I consider hopping off the wagon and finding her. But it's bad enough to have let down Grandmother, Father, and Cosie, and I'm not ready to revisit the humiliation of my failure so soon. I remain on the buckboard. For the remainder of the journey, I pump my legs and only fall back against the side of beef once.

Mirror Lake House is bustling when we arrive. The compact building sits right on the lakeshore, with a dance floor that extends out over the water. Grandmother keeps me in tow as Mrs. Howard guides us past tourists enjoying the view from the porch.

"There is so much to do," Mrs. Howard says once we reach the kitchen. She picks up a brightly colored paper lantern. "These must be set on the dance floor. There is also dough to be rolled and filled for pies, and of course we'll need more trout." She turns to me. "Delia tells me you enjoy fishing."

"I sure do. Only I didn't bring a pole," I say.

"I'm sure Captain Howard has one you may borrow."

Grandmother places a gentle hand on my shoulder. "Florence and I shall help with the lanterns."

I groan. Assisting with decorations is precisely the kind of fussy chore I hate. Rolling out pies would be tolerable, because at least I could sneak a bite of dough now and then. Fishing would be too much of a pleasure, being precisely what I'd want to do anyway. I cannot refuse. Lanterns, it is.

I take the lantern from Mrs. Howard's hand. It's not her fault I'm in this position. "How would you like them?"

She describes her vision of the Chinese lanterns strung from the railing of the dance floor. I suppose it will look nice, if one happens to enjoy parties. By the time Grandmother and I are ready to begin, the boxes of lanterns have already been unloaded from the wagon and sit piled on the dance floor. We set to work.

Each box contains four lanterns, delicately packaged in stiff paper. The red silk of each lantern is smooth and cool, despite the day's building heat, and even I must admit that they are an extravagance unlike any seen in Yosemite before.

"These are finer than the porcelain bathtubs at the Cosmopolitan!"

Grandmother gives a ladylike snort. "Only a person who prefers bathing in the river would say that."

I nearly drop a lantern.

"Come now. I may be old, but I am capable of humor."

"If you say so."

She offers me a bemused smile, and then we continue our work. Half Dome is visible from the dance floor and pulls incessantly at my attention. Every few minutes my eyes flit to the arc of the summit, the black line trailing down its face like tears and the slanted ledge of my misadventure. Each glance brings a new pang in my chest.

"What are you looking at?" Grandmother asks as she ties another lantern to the railing.

"I was thinking of my first memory of Mirror Lake," I fib.

She pauses, her hands lingering on the string. "What were you, two years of age? Perhaps three?"

"I only remember sitting on Mother's lap. I think we were having a picnic."

Grandmother nods thoughtfully and resumes tying. "Elvira drew the lake in her sketchbook. She was quite adept at rendering the reflections on its surface."

I pick up another lantern and lace the cord through its brace. Mother would have enjoyed decorating, and an enterprise such as this feels strange without her. Unexpected melancholy washes over me. Is Mother happy that she left us? If given the chance, would she make the same choice again?

"The lake is shallower than when I first saw it," Grandmother continues. That was twelve summers ago, the same year I was born. "Each year the creeks bring in more sand."

"Grandmother," I say quietly, still thinking about my mother. "Do you ever want things to go back to the way they were?"

"I've found it's best not to look back." Her voice is unexpectedly soft. "When I said you weren't a little girl anymore, Florence, I meant it. And neither do you live in the same world in which you grew up. Yosemite may still host the granite walls and rivers of your childhood, but it too is changing . . ." She trails off. Her gaze searches beyond the lake, and she seems lost in memory. Then she pulls out another lantern. "You may resist all you like, but this is your new world."

I rest my head against the railing, and my melancholy

fades a little as she starts to hum. When I begin to hum along with her, she looks up with a surprised smile on her face. I grin back.

We are nearly finished working when Sally Ann steps onto the dance floor with a tray of lemonade.

"Thank you, Sally Ann." I take a sip. "It's quite hot out."

"You're welcome." She pours Grandmother a glass. "Here you are, Miss Florantha."

"What a lovely treat, Sally Ann. But fetch another glass from the kitchen, would you, please?" Grandmother says. "You should have some as well."

Sally Ann glances toward the porch, where a tourist couple watches us. She shakes her head.

"Nonsense." Grandmother stands. "I shall get you a glass. You may sit with Floy."

Sally Ann doesn't sit, but neither does she abandon me to the decorations. She picks up Grandmother's forgotten lantern and ties it to the railing.

Without you, I want to say, *I'd be stuck on that ledge!*

But the words will not come—my embarrassment is still too great. I pick up another lantern and work next to her.

She tilts her head in the direction of Half Dome. "What is your plan for returning to Tissiack?" she says.

I hesitate. Everything happened so fast—the climb, the return, the punishment—I've hardly had time to count my blessings, let alone plot another attempt at the mountain.

"Or do you mean not to?" she asks.

"Of course not! I mean, yes!" I set my lantern down and take a deep breath to clear my thoughts. "Yes, I mean to try again."

She picks up my lantern and hands it back to me. "It is like falling off a horse. You must get back on."

Sally Ann would know. She's the only person who can beat me when the Valley residents host horse races. "Will you help me?" I ask. "You're a good climber."

She looks up from her knot, her eyebrows pinched together. "But I do not want to climb Tissiack."

"You don't have to. Just help me get better at climbing."

Before she can respond, Grandmother returns with a third glass and fills it with lemonade before handing it to Sally Ann.

"Thank you," Sally Ann says. She takes a tentative sip, grimaces, then gulps down the rest before setting the glass on the tray. "If you need anything else, Miss Florantha, just send Floy to find me."

Grandmother's eyes trail after her. "As I was saying, a changing world demands that we change with it. Whether we desire to or not."

I follow her gaze. "What does that have to do with Sally Ann?"

She picks up another lantern. "You're not the only one whose world is changing. It might do you good to remember that."

SIXTEEN

After three days, the party preparations are finally complete. Lanterns have been hung, pies and bread baked. Mrs. Howard left no detail unconsidered, and surely it will be a centennial to remember. Outside Leidig's Hotel, the horses stand hitched to our open-air stage. Yet I am not ready, even knowing how lovely the decorations look and how delicious the food will surely taste, not to mention how much work I put in at Grandmother's side. If only the dress she has provided didn't frighten me.

There are *bows*!

Cosie's already wearing her new dress, complete with ruffles, and is helping Willie tuck his shirt in. "It's a party dress," she says. "It's supposed to have adornments."

I eye the garment, as if it might jump off the bed at me. "Yes, well, these adornments are hideous."

She huffs impatiently. "Why don't you cut them off, then?"

I rush from the room and down the stairs. I'm back, moments later, with Grandmother's sewing scissors in hand.

Cosie's eyes widen. "What did you tell her they were for?"

"I didn't say anything. She and Mrs. Leidig are on the porch, talking with the travelers from France."

I pick up the dress. Its navy-and-gray-striped silk taffeta is far from the worst of fabrics I've been forced to wear, but the bows must go. I snip carefully at the stitching, and one by one the bows fall to the floor.

Cosie leans over my shoulder to inspect my work. "She'll notice."

"I do not care," I reply, pulling at a remnant thread. "It still looks fancy enough. You've saved me from looking like a trussed peacock."

She laughs. "I'm not so sure you still won't!"

I ignore her and pull off my pinafore. Then she helps me slide the taffeta dress over my head.

"It fits you nicely," Cosie says, buttoning up the back.

I take a few steps. "I can move my legs. That's a start."

"You're not climbing a mountain in it! Are you?"

That stings. "No."

I check her curls one last time, and we head downstairs. Father is already mounted on Leidig's big gray horse, which he's ridden since we arrived. In the stage, Willie sits at Grandmother's side and pulls at the tie around his neck. Cosie climbs up next to them, and I am forced to squeeze onto the last bench seat with the couple from France. Most of the Valley's tourists are expected at the Howards', but a few will remain at the Cosmopolitan Saloon for billiards and a strong drink.

Just before Mirror Lake House comes into view, the Frenchwoman lifts her hand and points. *"Regardez!"*

A small party of Indians are walking in the trees just beyond the road. I crane my neck to see but cannot spot Sally Ann with them. I'd been hoping she would come. We'd talked often enough at the Howards' but always in the company of Grandmother with no chance to speak of Half Dome. I slouch back onto the seat.

The woman covers her nose. "Our guidebook said their village is unsightly and has a most unpleasant odor."

Tourists have voiced this kind of view before, so I should not be surprised. Even Mr. Muir did not travel with Indians and claimed they were unclean.

"That's not true," I say.

The Frenchwoman shifts her gaze to me. "Does it not offend you, how close they are to the hotels? Tell me, why are they allowed to stay?"

A sour tang fills my mouth. "They stay because they live here. The Valley is their home."

Her husband tilts his head to better see through the trees. "Perhaps we could arrange a visit to their village. For some time, I have been interested in observing a teepee up close."

"The Indians here live in umachas, not teepees," I say.

His eyes widen. "Well, even more intriguing."

"If you insist on going, you shall do it alone," the Frenchwoman says through tight lips.

Grandmother will know how to talk to these people. Peering around the guests in front of me, I search her out. She's holding Willie's hands on her lap, likely to keep them out of his nose, and she doesn't seem to have heard our conversation. "Grandmother!" I call. When she doesn't turn around, I address the couple. "My grandmother lived with the Ojibwa in Wisconsin for a time."

The Frenchman leans closer. "Was she a missionary?"

"Yes," I say.

His wife nods approvingly. "That is most admirable work."

I consider calling to Grandmother again, because in truth I know little about her experience, but the couple has moved on to making predictions about the party. Their awful words do not abandon me as quickly.

At Mirror Lake House, I make my way to the kitchen in search of Sally Ann. Instead, I find Johnny. He's steadying a chair leg while Captain Howard hammers it back into place. Johnny nearly drops the leg when he sees me. I've avoided him since that day in the boulder field, both because I failed and because he'd been right. I escape the room before he can speak to me.

Bonfires dot the lakeshore even though twilight is hours away. I skirt around the people already enjoying the fires until I find a rock with a clear view of Half Dome and its near perfect reflection in the lake below. From here, it's obvious just how pitiful my attempt had been. I'd barely climbed above the tops of the trees. Trying so hard had gotten me nowhere.

Once, I'd felt free. Determined. Invincible.

And now?

I feel caught. Uncertain. Inadequate.

"Don't taunt me," I say to the mountain.

I scatter a handful of sand into the water and watch as the reflection blurs into nothingness. Perhaps Grandmother was right. Perhaps holding on too tightly to the way things used to be is making me feel this way.

I look up again at Half Dome, but it has no answer.

Then I see Cosie walking along the shoreline, dragging a stick in the sand at the water's edge. She slows to squeeze between two bushy willows, and then carefully arranging her skirt, she perches on a log next to my rock. "It's beautiful, isn't it?"

"Yes. It truly is."

"I'm sorry that you didn't make it," she says. "I never got to say that, but I've been thinking it."

"Why're you sorry?"

"Because you wanted something and didn't get it."

"It's not your fault. I still want it, you know."

She looks down at her hands. "There's something I want, even though I won't get it."

"You'll make a great teacher someday, Cosie."

When she looks up, her eyes are wet. "I want Mother to live with us again."

If only I could give that to her. Instead, I reach for her hand and tap once.

A voice calls out my name. At first, I cannot tell where it is coming from, and then I see Johnny running toward me through the trees. "Floy!" he calls again.

He's panting when he reaches us and leans back against a tree to catch his breath. "We have to hurry."

"What's wrong?"

"Just come on."

He grabs my hand, and then we're racing past the bonfires back to Mirror Lake House. Out on the dance floor a small crowd has formed, with Father standing at its head. We are still far enough away that I cannot hear what he is saying. I squeeze past the French couple, Cosie and Johnny right behind me, and stop at Grandmother's side.

"What's happening?" I stand on my tiptoes to see.

"It seems your father is about to make an announcement," she says.

Father beams at the crowd. "Not nine months ago, by skill, unswerving perseverance, and personal daring, our own George Anderson first ascended the summit of the peak towering above us. The view atop is said to be without rival on earth."

Gooseflesh races up my arms. My dream!

Father continues. "And tomorrow, joined by these two brave souls from Manchester, England"—he gestures to a man in a simple suit and a woman who blushes at the attention—"I shall make my own climb of Half Dome."

Cosie reaches for my hand, but it hangs limp in hers. I remain frozen in place as Father lifts his chin triumphantly and scans the applauding crowd. Then his eyes meet mine, and before I can stop myself, I shout, "No!"

All eyes turn from him to me. Father takes a step toward me, but I spin away and push through the crowd. Once clear of the dance floor, I flee into the darkening woods, past the main building of Mirror Lake House and toward the ice house, where I can hide in the shadows.

Johnny reaches me before I get there. "Floy, wait!"

I stop but don't turn around.

"I know how much you wanted this."

Not wanted.

Want.

I slump back against a tree and press my hands into my eyes. "I've wanted to climb Half Dome since as long as I can remember. I've wanted this before you ever stepped foot in Yosemite Valley!"

He comes a little closer, and I jump to my feet.

After all that's happened this week—my failure on the mountain, how close I came to being sent back, the days spent fussing over boring decorations, not to mention this *dress*, the French people, and my own father's announcement—all I want is to be left completely alone. "I don't want your pity, Johnny Boitano. I don't want you to follow me around, and I certainly don't want to be your friend."

Shock ripples across Johnny's face. He steps backward, trips over a root, and smacks his head against the ground.

I rush over to him. "Man alive, I didn't mean it! Are you okay?"

He twists his head to avoid looking at me but nods. I reach out to help him up just as Father and Cosie step into the clearing. Father strides toward us and pulls me away.

"Ouch—let go!" I cry.

His grip does not lessen until we are across the clearing from Johnny, who is slowly getting to his feet with Cosie's help. Father stops and says through gritted teeth, "Florence, what's come over you?"

"I was helping him!"

He releases my arm. "Not this. Your outburst."

A twinge of regret awakens in me. I ignore it. I am too hurt.

"Why would you spoil the party?" he asks.

"Because of *you*!" I shout as my anger bursts free. "Did you ever once consider bringing me along?"

"Of course I considered it." He drags a hand over his bearded face. "But, Florence, what if something happened to you?"

"Don't you think I can do it?"

His silence tells me all I need to know.

"I cannot risk it," he finally replies with glistening eyes. He takes a deep breath before pulling me into his arms. His jacket smells like tobacco and pine trees, and I press my nose against the fabric. Then I catch myself and release him.

"*Please,*" I plead as Cosie comes to stand next to me. "Take me with you."

"The decision is made. Now I must get back to the celebration." He touches Cosie on the cheek and then heads back toward the dance floor.

My chin begins to shake, and I clench my jaw to keep from crying. Then Cosie grabs my hand, and my tears slip free. Father knows of my desire to climb Half Dome and does not consider me fit to accomplish it.

My sister and Johnny watch me cautiously, but their pity is unbearable. I wipe roughly at my eyes.

"Well," I say. "You two were right. Even Father thinks the climb is too difficult for me."

"Oh, Floy," Cosie says. "He doesn't mean it that way."

"Father always speaks plainly."

She knows I am right, and she doesn't respond.

"I vow to think of Half Dome no more," I say to them. "It's for the best."

SEVENTEEN

It's no use. Everything reminds me of Half Dome. Every boulder and water-streaked cliff, every glance at Cosie or Johnny, and every tourist party mounting up for an excursion. Even the deer trotting through the meadows at dusk remind me of returning home defeated. Father will be gone the better part of two days, and it's all I can do to keep my mind occupied in his absence.

The first day passes quickly. Mrs. Leidig finds odd jobs for me. I carry baskets of dirty clothes to Flores' Laundry, scrub dishes, pull clumps of matted fur from her dog, and run messages to and from the telegraph at Folsom Bridge. No task is refused, as long as it keeps me busy.

The second day begins with the walk to the north side of the Valley for school, when I must look away from the mighty crag itself, and it continues to drag until the final minutes of our geography lesson. After Ida releases us, Delia invites me to the Mirror Lake House.

Cosie claps her hands. "We're going to learn French from Madame Arnaud."

It takes me a moment to realize that Cosie is referring to the same woman who'd made rude comments about Indians on the ride to the centennial. I clutch my lunch pail and shake my head. "Mrs. Leidig's expecting me."

Cosie frowns. "I'm beginning to think you aren't fun anymore!"

I do not deny her claim. "You go on. I'll tell Grandmother where you are. Thank you for inviting me, Delia."

"Are you sure, Floy?" she replies. It's usually Cosie who's telling Grandmother where I've gone running off to, not the other way around.

I avoid her gaze. Delia must think I'm avoiding her. In truth, I'm avoiding her house, for it offers too many views of Half Dome. "I'm sure."

I plod my way back from school to Leidig's Hotel, kicking small rocks along the road. When I arrive, Grandmother waves to me from a rocking chair. I sit down on the edge of the porch and pull out the remains of my roast mutton lunch. "Where's Willie?"

"With the chickens, no doubt."

I start to stand. "I'll help him."

"Stay, Florence." Her furrowed brow suggests that she's

stewing over something. I take a bite of mutton, but there is little pleasure in eating it. After a few long minutes, Grandmother clucks her tongue. "You have been working hard lately."

"Mrs. Leidig seems to need the help."

"I know she appreciates it. As did Mrs. Howard. Perhaps now you might find Johnny or your sister."

I see what she is trying to do, but with Father's imminent return—and equally anticipated success—little will cheer me up. "Johnny is helping his father with the saddle horses, and Cosie has gone to Delia's house. Today they're learning French from Madame Arnaud."

"Are they really?"

"Yes."

Her mouth turns down at the corners, and I wonder if she's about to confide how much she dislikes people like the Arnauds. Instead she says, "You have not seemed yourself since your . . . excursion."

Grandmother is right. After the events of the past week, I'm as miserable as I was in San Francisco.

I'm a knife, misused and poorly honed.

I am becoming dull.

"When I said you must change, this is not what I imagined." Her eyes are filled with pity, just as Cosie's and Johnny's were that awful night. I cannot bear it any more now than I could then.

"I'm fine, Grandmother. I'd best find Willie. You know

how he can take his job as chicken master a bit too far."

Grandmother stands before I can. "I shall see to Willie. You should go for a walk."

"But I want to see him."

"You may see him at supper. For now, be gone."

At first, I wander with no specific destination. I am definitely heading west—away from Half Dome. The trail alongside the Merced River shifts from sand to grass to washed-out roots and back to sand. I trace my hand along the tips of the horsetail plants on the river's edge and stare up at the cliffs. Beneath them, I am insignificant as an ant.

Perhaps the dream of an ant doesn't matter.

I trudge on, following the twists and bends of the river toward Folsom Bridge. Ahead, a party of riders rests in the shade, and thinking to avoid them, I turn back only to stop in my tracks.

Half Dome.

A storm mounts behind its rounded summit, dark thunderheads building in layers. The sight feels like an omen. Inside my heart, a twin storm rages. I want this dream so intensely and yet have only found misery in it. I turn away.

A weasel leads me across a downed log to the opposite side of the river, and I move quickly. Then the umachas of Sally Ann's village wink into view through the trees.

A few children play in the shade of a black oak. An older woman with gray hair cropped like Sally Ann's sorts acorns in a flat basket. Next to her sits Sally Ann's mother, May, with an unfinished, bowl-shaped basket filling her lap. A tidy pile of redbud stems and willow roots, dried and cured, scraped and sized, rests by her side. She selects a strip of redbud and, squinting, wraps it around the frame of the basket before working the strip back through a small gap in the weaving.

Satisfied with her work, she looks up. "Hello, Floy." She gestures with her head toward the ground next to her, and I sit.

"Hi, Miss May. I'm here to see Sally Ann. Is she here?"

May wets a piece of willow root on her tongue to soften it and continues weaving. "She's working at the Howards'."

I'm not ready to head back to Leidig's. "May I wait here for her?"

"Of course," May replies.

I help Sally Ann's grandmother sort out the acorns that have holes in them, a sign that a brown beetle has hatched inside the shell and eaten the mealy nut. The remaining unblemished acorns will go to a granary for storage. Later, Sally Ann's grandmother will crack open the nuts and pound them into flour. Then she will pour cold and hot water over the flour, leaching it of acids. Only then can it be cooked into the delicious acorn patties Sally Ann shares with Cosie and me. Eventually, I tire of sorting acorns and instead help the younger children climb in the low branches of the oak. We are studying a camouflaged spider that jumps across the bark in spurts when Sally Ann appears.

"Floy!"

"Hey, Sally Ann." I hop from my branch and one at a time return the children to the ground. "Come with me to the creek?"

Sally Ann first greets her grandmother and mother, asks about their work, and shares news of her own day. As we leave for the creek, something awakens in me, and I rush back to the women under the tree.

"Thank you," I say to them.

Sally Ann's grandmother clasps my hand and then waves us off.

I follow Sally Ann up the babbling creek until a rock rolls beneath me and my foot slips into the creek. I suck in a breath as my other foot slides in, too.

"Blazes, that's cold!"

I slosh angrily onto the bank and start unlacing my boots.

"That's one way to cool off!" Sally Ann says.

"It's not funny."

She raises her eyebrows.

"Fine," I groan. "It is funny."

She stretches out on the stony bank next to me. I remove my stockings and wring them out, watching the drips fall in dark splotches onto a rock. Sally Ann has begun tossing pebbles into the shallow water, and I watch until my drying feet start to itch and my doubts take over again.

Wet stockings and boots would never have kept me from an adventure before. I can't even handle a simple creek walk. Maybe I should return to the hotel. Check on Willie. Mrs. Leidig will want help serving supper. And Grandmother will no doubt have words of wisdom that I don't know what to do with.

I make no move.

What am I waiting for?

"Sally Ann," I say, as if she might have the answer.

Her eyes are clear and open. Of all the people I know in the Valley, she's the only one who's always offered me encouragement, rather than words of caution. She hasn't asked me to be different. She didn't judge me on the slabs below Half Dome, and her face shows no judgment now.

Sally Ann glances at my bare feet and then asks, "Are you ready?"

I will not close myself off to everything that makes me *me*. I stand and toss my boots over my shoulder.

"I'm ready."

EIGHTEEN

Father's return is as I expected. After a rich dinner, he lectures in the parlor to all who will listen.

"The top is an astonishing expanse of nearly ten acres," he begins. "There are three species of pine as well as a variety of shrubs and grasses. Why, there's even a few chipmunks and grasshoppers who have made their own claims on the summit."

The crowd chuckles at his joke. I try my best to look uninterested, lingering near the door as I am, as if something more enticing could pull me away. In truth, I gobble up every word and offer them to my hungry dream.

In the morning, I skip Father's repeat performance and venture out of Yosemite Village, making my way to the mouth of Indian Cañon. There is no school today, on account of it being Sunday, and I'm off to meet Sally Ann.

The rising sun has not yet crested the Valley walls when I reach the bridge near Father's old hotel, and I blow into my cupped hands to warm them. I occupy myself by watching the river swirl and tumble over its rocky bottom. We hadn't chosen a destination, but Vernal Fall pulls at me. Hiking on the South Fork Cañon trail, which ultimately leads to Half Dome, might only add to my misery, but the fall is beautiful and deserving of a visit on its own.

When Sally Ann arrives, I tell her my idea. "I haven't yet been up there this summer."

"I have no money," she says.

Both the ladders to the top of the waterfall and the horse trail that travels around charge tolls. I shrug. "Me neither. We don't have to go all the way."

Mrs. Leidig provided a loaf of crusty bread for the outing, and I tear it into chunks and pass a piece to Sally Ann. We eat as we walk. A light rain last night has dampened the road, and the early hour means no saddle trains will force us to the side. The stillness recalls the days when summer tourists numbered in the hundreds, not thousands. Once the sun fully rises, the saddle trains will surely pass us by, but for now the roads are quiet and dust-free. I am content.

I skip a few steps, then match Sally Ann's quick pace again. "It's a beautiful morning."

She makes as if to throw her bread at me. "Every morning is beautiful."

"Sally Ann?" I say.

"Hmm?"

"Do you remember what it was like before?"

"Before what?"

I don't know what I'm asking exactly. There are so many befores. Before I moved away. Before the carriage roads opened and more tourists flooded the Valley, with guidebooks in hand. Before I was expected to grow up and leave my childhood and dreams behind. But these befores are mine, not Sally Ann's. She has her own befores.

I glance at her as she brushes a stray hair from her cheek. If only those French people could see Sally Ann as I do. She is kind and funny and true.

"What do you dream of?" I ask.

Sally Ann slows and then stops in the road.

"What do you want more than anything?"

Her eyes shine fiercely. "I want to be a weaver. Like my mother and grandmother."

"That future sounds likely enough, doesn't it?"

"There is much to learn. And I worry I will not be good enough."

I know the feeling more than I ever have, and yet I cannot bear to see it hinder her. "You mustn't give up. It's too important."

She holds my gaze a moment and then turns back toward Yosemite Village. "Someone is on the road," she says.

"It's Johnny."

I've not seen much of him since my vow, and today I've little interest in more caution and warnings. I take Sally Ann's hand, tempted to step off the road before he sees us. However, the last time I tried to avoid Johnny, I got stuck on a ledge. "Hey, Johnny," I say as he walks up. "Following me again?"

A flush rises in his cheeks. "What? No!"

"I was only joking."

He toes the dirt with his shoe. "I . . . uh . . . Where are you going, then?"

I laugh. "You sure are predictable!"

"We are hiking to the falls," Sally Ann says.

"Oh."

I study him as he stares at the ground. "Would you like to join?"

He rubs the back of his neck. "I don't know."

"Then why follow us?"

"I wasn't . . ." His shoulders slump. "I do want to join! It's just . . ."

I nudge his knee gently, but he won't look at me. "Tell us, Johnny."

"Well . . . I . . ."

"Please?"

"I, um, I don't think I can keep up."

"What do you mean?"

"You're so quick, and you, too, Sally Ann. It's hard to be around sometimes."

"Now, don't get all mad," he adds quickly, just as I'm about to open my mouth. "I know you can't help being strong and fast, but I guess it's hard for me to be bested by a girl." The words erupt from him, and he blinks.

"I don't know what to say."

He drags a hand through his hair. "I just want to be friends again. For real. Like before."

So that's his "before." I hold out my hand, and he takes it.

The three of us walk side by side down the road. Ahead, the path narrows and inclines on its way toward Vernal Fall. The river will steepen with the trail, causing the water to flow more swiftly and with more force. "Let's cross here, before it gets too steep."

We hop along the rocks and logs over the water, and this time my feet remain dry.

Sally Ann leads the way as the footing changes from leaves and sticks to rocks and boulders. Heart racing, I clamber over them, using my hands and feet. When Johnny stops, I climb back down and offer him the last chunk of bread. "Here."

"Heavens, you two are fast." He's breathing too hard to eat straightaway. Once he catches his breath, he chews a bite of the bread and then shoves the rest into his mouth. "Let's go."

"For someone slower than the girls, you sure are taking it well," I say.

"I've had a lot of practice."

We rejoin Sally Ann and continue up the talus, helping one another over the steeper sections. Sally Ann tells us better ways to shift our weight and place our feet as we climb.

"It looks clear over there," she says, guiding us toward a break in the bay trees.

The opening leads to a small shelf of rock. To the east, Liberty Cap rises like a smaller version of Half Dome. In the thickly forested cañon below, the Merced River drops over Vernal Fall's broad, sharp edge. The flow may be weaker in July than during the spring, but it still takes my breath away. Then Sally Ann points up the cañon to where the top of Nevada Fall is just visible. I've looked down on this cañon many times from Glacier Point, but never considered it was possible to see both waterfalls from below.

"Look!" Johnny says. "Yosemite Fall makes three!"

I turn to see. On the far side of the Valley, the upper and lower falls are thin wisps of water against more than two thousand feet of cliff.

"Four," Sally Ann replies. "If you count Yosemite as two."

I twist back around toward Vernal, and my eye catches something. "Five!" I point to a trickle of water to the west of Vernal and Nevada. "Don't forget Illilouette."

We take turns steadying each other as we spin in circles and try to make the five waterfalls merge into one. It's a pointless game, but we play until the dizziness becomes too much and then settle down on the ledge with our backs against the cliff. Johnny whistles, and Sally Ann twirls a bay leaf between her fingers. I pull out my granite rock and rub my thumb against the crystals.

Together we discovered a secret, special place, and my heart hasn't felt this full since I galloped back into the Valley. Hope seems impossible to resist. This is not San Francisco. I cannot simply run away from my dream. I cannot give up.

I turn to my friends. "There is something I need to do. Will you help?"

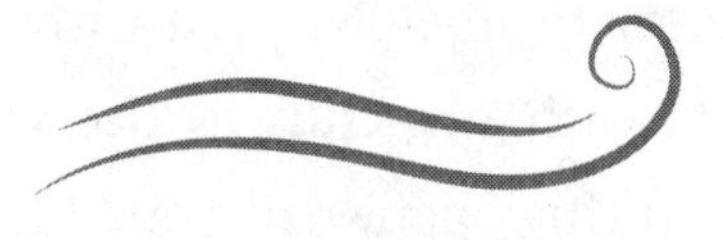

NINETEEN

In the blink of an eye, July becomes August, and the dry days of late summer pass without much fanfare until the middle of the month when my birthday arrives.

Blazes! Twelve at last!

It's Saturday, and Grandmother has arranged for a riding tour up the Four-Mile Trail. The trail leaves from directly behind Leidig's Hotel and ends at Glacier Point, an overlook on the Valley rim where there is a view far into the high country. Neither Cosie nor I have been to the rim yet this summer, and while we help Mrs. Leidig pack lunches, we pinch each other in excitement.

As Cosie wraps the final plum pie in muslin, I sneak up and reach for her ticklish side.

She sidles away. "No, you don't!"

I race to the far side of the table and stick out my tongue. "You can't catch me!"

She pouts dramatically. "Not fair—my hands are full!" Then she points with her chin to the saddlebag on the table. "Here, hold this open, will you? I hope this doesn't burst," she says as she carefully sets the pie inside. I strap the bag closed, and we head outside, where Grandmother and Father wait with the horses.

Father holds his arms out. "Happy birthday again! My dearest Floy."

My secret plan with Sally Ann and Johnny has helped ease my frustration with him, and I step into his embrace. He leans back and considers me.

"Do I look a year older?"

"Every year." He pulls out a large paper package from his saddlebag and hands it to me. "I was going to wait to give you this, but you might want it for our ride."

The paper falls away to reveal a brimmed hat, just like his. I set it immediately on my head. "Father! It's wonderful." This hat shields my face far better than any floppy bonnet. Then I notice there are only three horses. "Grandmother, are you not coming?"

"Of course I am, Florence." She adjusts her own hat. "Are you? You're not wearing your riding clothes."

I smooth my hands over my dress. "I thought maybe"—I lean in so only she can hear—"I might see how growing up feels."

"That is most mature of you, Florence."

The pride in her voice makes me stand a little taller. "Thank you," I say, "for planning this outing for my birthday."

We are still one horse too few. I turn to Cosie. "Does that mean you're not coming?"

She bites back a smile as her eyes catch on something over my shoulder.

I turn to see Johnny walking toward us, leading two horses. The bay I recognize, as we often visit his father's stables to feed apples to the horses, and Johnny claims this one is the best of the barn. The other is an unfamiliar, scrawny black mare with flaring nostrils. As he passes her reins to me, she leans close and nips me in the leg.

"Ouch!" I squeal. "You're worse than Cosie!" I grab hold of her bridle so she can't bite me again.

"Happy birthday, Floy," Johnny says.

"You mean, she's mine?"

"For the rest of the summer. She's, uh, not real popular with the tourists, so my father said you could have her."

The mare nips the air and tries to jerk her head free from my grip.

"I can see why. What's her name?"

He scrunches his face. "I don't recall that she has one."

I give her thick neck a good scratching, and her upper lip curls. Then she shakes her entire body, releasing a cloud of dust. "I love her, Johnny. Thanks."

"Don't let her get the bit between her teeth. She bucks."

It takes both Johnny and Father to hold the mare still while I mount. As I gather up the reins, her ears flatten against her head.

"She's feisty," Cosie says. Her own mount's head hangs as if it's asleep.

"I shall call her Radish."

We strike off up the trail, falling in behind a saddle train led by Manuel, the son of Mr. Flores, who owns the laundry. Unlike the zigzag trail into the Valley, this path is well graded, and the mules and horses gain the trail quickly. We stop to rest the horses at Union Point, which provides a stunning view of the pointed peak of Sentinel Rock and El Capitan beyond.

"Radish likes me," I say. I offer her a nibble of plum pie, which she snatches up eagerly.

"Sure, she does," Cosie replies.

"She hasn't bucked me off."

Johnny leans back against a rock and tips his hat over his face. "I don't think she's really tried yet."

I push his foot with mine, and he topples over, grinning.

"Time to go," Father calls out from the shade of a towering pine.

We mount up, and while we ride, I relish the feeling of Radish's muscles moving beneath me.

Then Cosie's horse trips and falls against Radish's rump.

Radish drops her head, and her back legs kick high into the air.

"Whoa!" I fly out of the saddle into a scrubby bush. "My ankle!"

I lean my head back into the bush and wait for the throbbing to subside. Then soft, whiskery lips brush against my forehead. My mare looms over me. "Why, Radish! You do care!"

Johnny leans against her shoulder to push her out of the way. "Are you all right?"

"I'm fine. Or I will be when I get out of this bush."

He offers me a hand, and together we manage to extract me from the scratchy branches. When I try to stand, pain shoots through my foot. Johnny catches my arm before I fall and guides me to Radish's side.

"Can you ride?"

I can ride. But walking? Climbing? I shove the thoughts down.

The remainder of the ride to the top of the Four-Mile Trail is subdued. Even Radish doesn't pin her ears back once. Hours drag on before the trail opens up, and there it is.

Half Dome!

How wondrous! What majestic beauty!

I cannot catch my breath.

The peak appears as if someone sliced through a granite mountain with a knife, leaving one round portion with a sheer face and nothing but an expanse of space for the other. It stands wondrously apart, unlike any of the other peaks beyond it. My dream of climbing to the top swells inside me, as if it were a living thing reminding me not to forget about it.

Radish stomps, sending a jolt through my ankle, but I welcome the distraction. Carefully, I dismount and loosen the girth to her saddle before limping toward the rest of my group. Johnny supports me as we make our way to the edge of the overlook and then helps me find a rock to rest on.

"I don't know," he says, rubbing his chin. "Half Dome doesn't look so big from here. It actually looks rather easy."

"Johnny Boitano, you cannot be serious! From here, it may look a simple task, but once you're up close it's all too clear that the rock is—" Then I see the smirk on his face, and he has to duck to avoid getting swatted.

When I'd asked Johnny and Sally Ann to help me prepare for another attempt at Half Dome, I'd been thinking more of practice scrambles. This seems shortsighted now. Perhaps I need laughter more than anything else.

TWENTY

Radish has become my constant companion. Without her, this past week would have seen me confined to the parlor, my injured ankle elevated on a pillow.

How intolerable!

Instead, I ride Radish everywhere. To school. To the base of Yosemite Falls. To my favorite fishing spot by the meadow near El Capitan. Most days, Johnny rides his horse with me.

One day after Ida releases us from school, Johnny and I strike out for a small meadow east of Sally Ann's village and just below the Royal Arches. Sally Ann is determined that I craft my own rope to affix to trees and granite blocks before reaching Mr. Anderson's rope.

"And you'll know how to repair your rope, if it breaks," she said. Though she surely has a point, I'd rather not consider any situation in which my rope might break on Half Dome.

We find her at the edge of a small marsh filled with waist-high Indian hemp plants. I tie Radish to a low branch. "Sorry we're late," I say.

Johnny points at Radish. "It's her fault. She wouldn't stop grazing."

"She'll be no good in a race," Sally Ann says. "You spoil her."

I shrug. "It makes her happy."

Johnny and I sit down in the grass next to Sally Ann. For our first lesson, she taught us how to crack the dried stalks of last year's plants into four long pieces. Then we separated the woody inner stem from the papery outer fibers that we'll use today to twist into twine.

Sally Ann pulls a clump of loose fibers from a basket next to her and divides it into two sections. "You first twist two strands of fibers separately and then tightly wrap the twisted strands around each other, like this. The curling holds them together."

The quick movements of her hands are mesmerizing.

I watch her a minute before pulling a handful out of the basket. After separating it into two, I begin rolling each strand as she directed until I feel the tension in the coils push at my fingers. Then I accidently release the strands, and all my work uncoils in a burst.

"Drat!"

"Try it like this," Sally Ann suggests, slowing her movements so I can see better.

I try again, this time managing to not lose my hold on the strands. When I have figured out the process enough that Sally Ann does not have to stop me midtwist, she picks up her own rope and works beside me.

I peek over at Johnny, whose strands look much tighter than mine.

"I guess there's something I *can* do better than you, Floy."

"I'm depending on this rope, so you'd better."

He pauses. "Why do you want it so much? Half Dome, I mean."

I set down my work. There is no clear answer—I simply want it—but I do know when the dream took root. "When I was five, Father tried to climb Half Dome. No one had ever attempted it before, but he was determined. He set out one morning with a man whose name I can't remember and a train of mules carrying rope. Mother had taken me and Cosie to Mirror Lake, where we played at the water's edge and talked about how Father was going to climb to the top. I kept imagining that I could see him up there."

"Did he make it?" Sally Ann asks.

I shake my head. "The rock was too smooth, and he came down." I realize now that Father must have been devastated. I close my eyes. "He wanted to be the first."

"Your father is a tough old man," Johnny says inspecting his twine. "But between the two, I'd say George Anderson has more grit."

The brawny Scotsman might look the part, but Father has more than enough grit. He built trails and roads, wrote countless articles and publications, all for his beloved Yosemite. I'd always imagined the same tenacity lived inside me. "Sometimes I'm afraid he's right. That I'm not strong enough to make the climb."

I pick my work back up to busy myself, but I can feel Johnny watching me.

"I'm afraid, just like you are," he says.

Sally Ann scoffs. "Now you want to climb Tissiack, too?"

"Ha! No." He pulls another clump of fibers from the basket and begins a new strand of twine.

"Then what are you afraid of? Besides being too slow."

"That I'll be stuck here forever, saddling horses and breathing dust," he says. "Yosemite is nice enough, but I really want to see the ocean and sail on a ship."

"Where would you go?" Sally Ann asks.

"Italy, where my grandparents are from."

I do not like the idea of him ever leaving, but who am I to deny him his dream when he is assisting my own? "Sally Ann, you won't ever leave, will you?"

Sally Ann's hands still. "I worry that someday there will no longer be a place for my family in this Valley."

As I take in the tension on her face, Grandmother's words come rushing back to me: *You're not the only one whose world is changing.* What would Yosemite be without Sally Ann and her family together under the black oak in their village? My chest feels empty at the thought, and I shudder.

"What's wrong?" asks Sally Ann.

"It's nothing. I'm just glad you're here."

"You can thank my mother! She taught me how to make rope."

We continue our task, and Johnny entertains us with a detailed comparison of Mrs. Leidig's plum pie and Mrs. Snow's elderberry one. After a while, I pull the length of twine through my fingers, checking for slack spots. Once I've confirmed that the only loose sections are minor, I hold up the twine in my hands. "How am I doing?"

Sally Ann's fingers still work a steady rhythm of twist and roll even as she looks up. She presses her lips together, clearly holding back a grin. "You're lucky Johnny has some skill."

"Is it that pathetic?" I say.

"Only a little," Johnny adds.

I smile. Once we're done making our own lengths of twine, which may take a week or more, we'll twist them all together into one bigger rope. If my attempt on Half Dome ultimately proves successful, it will only be because I trusted these two with my dream.

TWENTY-ONE

Knowing a bucket of grain awaits her, Radish canters the entire way to the stables. After giving her a good brushing, I return to the Leidigs'. Grandmother is in the parlor with Father. "Florence, come sit."

After I've settled onto a chair opposite her, she says, "Your father and I were just discussing the fact that we have barely six weeks left before our return to San Francisco."

"I know."

She sips at her tea. "I should like to climb Half Dome before we go."

So many people have surprised me in recent weeks—including Grandmother—that I hardly react. But Father's jaw drops.

"Florantha," he says. "I speak with experience that the climb is quite difficult."

She waves a hand. "If I should fail, then at least I'll have tried."

I sit up straighter. She's looking at Father, but it feels as if she's speaking directly to me.

"So, I shall attempt it," she continues. "And I should like, James, for you to guide me."

"I suppose I owe it to you."

"You do."

"I'll speak to George in the morning." Then he opens a book and starts reading.

"Well, then," Grandmother says. "I must see if Mrs. Leidig needs assistance with preparing dinner." On her way out, she meets my eye and winks!

Then I'm alone with Father, but it feels as if Grandmother remains here with me. Could it really be as simple as she makes it seem? I must follow her lead. Should I fail, then at least I'll have tried.

"Father," I start. "I should like to speak with you."

Father draws on his pipe. His eyes remain on his page, but I can tell he's not actually reading. "I'm guessing you'd like to join in on your grandmother's tour?"

"Why, yes. That is exactly what I meant to say."

He slides a marker into his book and closes it. "Half Dome is no trifling adventure."

"I understand." I swallow the lump in my throat and struggle to find Grandmother's poise. "It's my dream."

"I know that now." He lifts his pipe to his lips, and smoke puffs from his mouth in gray clouds. "Go on."

His silent gaze presses on me—he doesn't think I can do it. I push the thought away and continue. "Ever since you first climbed it, it has been on my mind." I tell him my memory of the picnic at Mirror Lake with Cosie and Mother, and of imagining him at the summit. "I tried it once."

He frowns. "What do you mean?"

"Do you remember the day I returned home in the dark?"

"As I recall it, you've done so on more than one occasion."

His lightheartedness buoys me. "My plan was to hike up beneath the face in order to gain the shoulder and Mr. Anderson's ropes from that direction. That way, no one would see me and try to stop me."

He leans forward. "And did you?"

I look down at my hands. "No."

"Well, that is no surprise." Thankfully, he doesn't press me for the details. Instead, he reaches for my hand and squeezes it. "You have time, Floy."

Father failed at first, and so had Mr. Anderson prior to his success. Failure did not stop them from trying again. "I am ready now," I say.

He taps my finger as Cosie does. "I see you protecting it, your ankle."

I sit up taller. "It's nothing."

He squeezes my hand once more and then sits back. "You truly desire this."

I nod. "I know now I cannot do it alone."

"I must be honest with you, Floy," Father says. "I have ascended many peaks, some of them with you, but there is no doubt that Half Dome is far and away the most challenging I've ever attempted."

My dream starts to sink like a stone in my stomach. I close my eyes.

He continues. "The rock is smooth, polished so by the glaciers, and there is little for one's hands to hold on to. To fall from such a height . . . Well, I am not eager to risk your life with such an endeavor. And I'm suspect that you, with your stubborn streak, will try it on your own again. It's crossed my mind to send you back to San Francisco."

The wake of my sunken dream threatens to tug my heart down with it.

"However," Father says before pausing. When I open my eyes, I can see that his are shining. He rests a hand tenderly on my shoulder.

"I know what it is to dream. And it seems as if my own ambitions have ensnared you as well. You may accompany us on horseback to where the trail hits the small dome at Half Dome's shoulder. After that, we shall see."

I cannot ask for more. I leap from my seat and throw my arms around his neck.

TWENTY-TWO

My hands shake as I tighten the girth on Radish's saddle. She twists her head around to nip me, but I swat her away. "Stupid mare." When her ears pin back, I soften. My head falls against her neck, and I scratch absently at the place where the bridle rubs against her ears. "I'm sorry, girl. It's just, I'm all wound up today."

After weeks of waiting first for my ankle to heal and then for drier skies, this morning we ride to Mr. Snow's hotel, La Casa Nevada. My ankle is much improved, and there's not a cloud in the sky. After spending the night at Snow's, we will make for the shoulder of Half Dome and the summit beyond. I could reach the top by tomorrow midday.

If Father concedes that I may join the summit party, that is.

I bury my face into Radish's mane. "I know I asked for this, my dear Radish, but sometimes it seems like too much."

This public attempt of Half Dome has resulted in more attention than even *I'd* like. While I rested my ankle in the parlor, Father talked me through the climb, step by slippery step. Grandmother insisted I eat an extra helping of trout to give me additional strength. Mr. Anderson, who will be guiding us, coached me on a practice climb of the leaning oak behind Black's Hotel, showing me how to properly weight my feet and hold the rope without burning the skin on my hands. By now I've imagined the details so many times, it's as if I've already completed the climb.

Radish tenses, and I turn to see Cosie. She's holding out my riding jacket.

"You left this in the dining room," she says.

I slip it on. "Thanks. Don't tell Grandmother I nearly forgot it. I wouldn't hear the end of it."

"What's that?" She points to my wrist.

Pulling back the sleeve of my jacket, I show her the bracelet of Indian hemp. "Sally Ann taught me and Johnny how to make rope. Mr. Anderson claims he has plenty, but I'm bringing it along anyway. And I decided to wear a piece of it for luck."

Cosie starts braiding Radish's forelock. "I'm glad for you." Her voice is so soft, I can barely hear it.

"Wait, Cos," I say. "Did you want to come with us?"

She shakes her head. "Perhaps once Mr. Anderson completes his stairway. And even if I did, I don't think Father or Grandmother could possibly handle the worry."

A laugh escapes me. "I know. They're acting as if I intend to climb El Capitan!"

Her eyes widen. "Do you think that's even possible?"

"Of course not. El Capitan is three thousand feet of smooth, vertical rock! Our climb is significantly shorter and not nearly as sheer."

She hugs me fiercely. "Remember, you are not Zanita," she says. "This is your story, not hers."

"My story," I repeat.

She runs back to the porch, where Willie is being comforted by Mrs. Leidig. Poor boy is being left behind again. I wave my hat in the air and steer Radish into line behind Grandmother. We take the wagon road to the Merced River cañon. Father and Mr. Anderson entertain the other member of our party, a Mr. Hamilton from San Francisco, with stories of their past ascents of Half Dome. I listen half-heartedly, pulling my jacket against me to ward off the morning chill. Radish prances and pulls at the reins.

I lay my palm against her neck. "Easy. Now's not the time for a gallop."

She continues to toss her head, as if she knows what awaits us. I don't blame her for being impatient. Grandmother rides at a snail's pace, and the striking of Radish's hooves against the hardened path winds me tighter.

This is really happening!

We pass the spot where I crossed the river with Sally Ann and Johnny. That day, with its five waterfalls and two true friends, showed me that my dream of summiting Half Dome is only one part of who I am. There are countless adventures to be had, secret places to discover. Someday I will have other dreams to reach for. Why, perhaps one day I'll stand at the top of Bridal Veil Fall! Calm spreads over me and even passes on to Radish, who begins to take the steepening trail more seriously.

At Grandmother's pace, it's nearing noon when we arrive at La Casa Nevada, which sits atop a rocky opening in the trees, with a view of Nevada Fall. After a summer of little rain, the water trickles over the edge in a thin stream.

Father takes Radish's reins. "You go inside and eat. Emily is expecting us."

He knows I can care for my own horse, but I am grateful nonetheless. "Thank you, Father." I give Radish a peck on the nose, pulling back before she can nip my face, and then head for the hotel.

Mr. Snow welcomes me at the door. "Why, Florence! It's almost midday!"

"Grandmother likes to take her time."

His smile is warm despite his lack of upper teeth. "If I'm not mistaken, there's pie in the making."

Inside, the parlor is quiet. Sitting by the fire is a stout woman—holding a copy of Mrs. Yelverton's novel. Its green cloth binding and gold lettering are a flame, drawing me in like a moth. Try as I might to put it behind me, the image of Zanita falling from the precipice of Half Dome is etched in my mind.

The woman glances up and smiles briefly before turning back to her book.

Blazes!

Cosie has insisted that *Zanita* is a fiction, and I want desperately to believe her. I also want to storm across this room, tear the book from this woman's hands, and rip it into a thousand insignificant pieces.

Instead, I step quietly through the parlor into the kitchen, where two ladies are rolling out circles of dough on a flour-covered table.

"Hello, Mrs. Snow," I say.

The older of the two looks up. Her brown hair is pulled tightly back into a low bun, and she wears a familiar scowl that contradicts her kindness. "Florence." She turns back to her work. "Albert tells me you're heading for South Dome."

She's using an earlier name for the mountain. For some reason, South Dome sounds less terrifying than Half Dome. Maybe I should consider using it. "Father is guiding my grandmother and me."

"Well, don't forget to sign the register before you leave, but you know that already." She lifts the circle of dough over a pie dish and presses it into place. "And there's fresh doughnuts on the sill."

I grab a doughnut for Father and am heading back through the parlor when I see the green book, abandoned on a side table. I glance back toward the kitchen before tucking the book under my arm.

Grandmother and I pass the afternoon resting on the porch before retiring early, but I do not sleep well. If only I could blame my wakefulness on the three pieces of elderberry pie I consumed at supper!

By morning, my body feels as if a hive of angry bees has taken it over. Father and Grandmother appear similarly high-strung, and our small party of five sets off from La Casa Nevada in a contemplative silence. A succession of hairpin turns on the trail brings us to the top of Nevada Fall and beyond to where the Merced River winds through Little Yosemite Valley. After a short rest to water the horses, we continue until the trail opens to a sweeping view of mountains beyond.

A cool pine-scented wind whips at my hair. We're as high as the northern rim of the Valley opposite us. Just a few hundred feet higher, and we'll be above the trees. Already it feels as if we're on top of the world, and yet the climb is still ahead.

How far I've come from the salty air and dusty roads of San Francisco!

"This is where we leave our mounts," Father says.

I take my time in tying Radish next to the others. "Don't fret," I say to her. "Father still has not decided. I might yet stay here with you."

She snorts, and snot flies from her nose. I wipe my cheek with my hand. "I love you, too."

When I rejoin the group, Mr. Anderson is talking through the process of climbing with the ropes and iron eyebolts that he hand-drilled into the rock almost a year ago. "You'll climb, keeping your feet flat against the rock, until you get to the next bolt. Then you can rest. Don't ever let go of the line."

My attention is so focused on the rope he's holding that, at first, I don't notice what's behind him.

Then I look up.

None of my preparations could have equipped me for what lies ahead. Not the warm afternoons with Sally Ann crossing talus slopes. Not the porch talks with Father.

A sweeping dome of gray granite rises sharply in front of me. Bushes and pines cling improbably to this shoulder of rock. The shoulder is an impressive peak in itself and steeper than the slabs I reached on my first attempt below Half Dome's vertical face. Yet, there are no ropes and bolts here. Only after this dome is climbed, without aid, can one attain the bottom of Mr. Anderson's lines and the true goal beyond. I can see the tip of the main summit—

the very top of the mountain—jutting into the turquoise sky like an iceberg. Gooseflesh rises on my arms.

This is the mountain the character Zanita climbed and fell from. The mountain I could die on.

This is Half Dome.

TWENTY-THREE

Father and I watch from the trees as Mr. Anderson guides Grandmother and Mr. Hamilton up the first series of ledges and cracks on the lower dome. Grandmother keeps pace, despite being sixty-five years old, and takes the gentlemen's hands when offered. I want to shout encouragement, but she's doing just fine without it.

"Are you ready?" Father asks.

I follow Grandmother's movements a seconds longer. Then a flush of heat rises in my body, and I hide my face in Radish's mane. Can I do this? What if I fail again? I shake my head, my thoughts too scattered for me to even speak.

"Very well, then." Father kisses my cheek, with neither disappointment nor relief on his face, and leaves me in

Radish's care. I peer over her neck, my hands gripping her mane, as he begins his own ascent, but my eyes fill with tears and I bury my head once more.

Radish's rhythmic breathing is like a balm to my agony, and I rest against her neck until the heat and tears subside. Now I stand alone, surrounded by trees, with the sloping path back to La Casa Nevada on the south side of me and a three-thousand-foot drop to Mirror Lake to the north. I was a fool to think I could climb Half Dome. Why, this right here is a destination all on its own! Yes, anyone could be satisfied with this sublime view!

So why am I not content with such beauty?

I press my forehead against Radish's, but she jerks back, knocking her bony cheek against my face. Then she bumps me—hard—and I stumble backward.

"Radish!"

She shakes her head, and when I step toward her, her ears flatten. Her "go away" expression is clear.

"Have it your way."

I turn my back to her and search the mountain, but the group has moved out of sight. My hands tighten into fists. The very thing I'd told Cosie I would do—find a way to join one of Father's parties to Half Dome—is slipping from my grasp. I shake my hands loose and untie my rope from Radish's saddle. Then I stride over to the base of the ledges and start climbing.

I may be a fool, but at least I'll be a fool who tried.

The way is not at all like my previous attempt underneath Half Dome's sheer face, and I quickly leave the forest and Radish behind. More than once, I toss my rope over a branch and haul myself higher, this time easily scaling smooth sections of rock. My ankle twinges every now and again, but I ignore it. I pause to catch my breath on ledges wide enough for several people, but otherwise move continuously, passing musty chinquapin shrubs and Jeffrey pines. Then, suddenly, I've gained the top of a steep slab. I struggle up and over a boulder to the flat shelf of the lower dome, not far from where Father and the others are resting.

I freeze.

Beyond the climbing party rises the iceberg. Impossibly, it is more massive than I ever could have imagined.

Smoother.

Grander.

The solid granite walls are without weakness and lead straight into the blue heavens above.

I cannot breathe.

This is my moment—yet all I can think is, *Mr. Anderson* climbed *this?*

Father rises from his perch on a rock. "Florence!"

"I changed my mind," I say when I can breathe again. "Is that all right?"

He breaks into a wide smile. "It's wonderful."

I coil my rope and settle it against my shoulder as we walk toward the bottom of our route. From this angle, the upper dome seems positively perilous. If one were to fall, they would tumble off the vertical cliff and down to the very slabs I tried to climb months ago. I place a hand against the rock to steady myself and close my eyes.

When I open them, I see that, up close, the rock is marvelous. I run my hand over the granite and barely a grain pulls at my skin. If Father and Mr. Muir and the geologists are correct, an enormous sheet of ice scoured and polished this face. The dark specks and pink and white crystals of the granite are unexpectedly familiar. I tuck away the thought for later and press my cheek against the rock.

A *thump-thump* rumbles through my ear.

Might Half Dome have a heartbeat?

Surely, I hear only the beating of my own heart, but at this moment, Half Dome and I are two halves of one heart.

Father calls me to the group. Then he demonstrates how we shall pull ourselves higher with Mr. Anderson's rope by picking up our feet and placing them flat against the rock. Every six feet or so, there are steel bolts that Mr. Anderson drilled into the rock face, on which we will rest. Demonstration over, I follow behind Father, grasping the thick rope with both hands and keeping my boots flat to maintain the most friction. It's like climbing a sheet of ice! With each step, I reach higher up the rope and soon establish a slow cadence. Reach, step. Reach, step. Where there is no bolt to stand upon, thin cracks and edges in the rock suffice. It is demanding work, and if not for Mr. Anderson's skillfully crafted line, there is no doubt none of us would be able to accomplish this. I make a point to thank him at the top.

Reach, step. Reach, step.

I look over my shoulder, past Grandmother below me, to the lower dome, and imagine sliding all the way down and crashing. It's easy to picture my crumpled, broken body.

Maybe I should retreat.

I could join Radish in the shade or ride back to La Casa Nevada. But that would be running away, and I will not do that anymore.

I tighten my grip on the rope and keep going.

Halfway to the summit, Grandmother calls out. Her boot has gotten stuck in one of the many cracks in the rock face. Mr. Anderson is aiding Mr. Hamilton and is too far away to help, as is Father. I must descend to her.

Going down means reversing my pattern. Find a firm stance for my feet, slide my hand lower on the rope, then repeat. The descent is only moderately easier than the ascent and vastly more terrifying. The rock slopes off on both sides, something I could not comprehend when climbing up. The V shape of Tenaya Cañon attracts my eye and guides my attention to the mountains beyond.

Blazes—this world is truly beyond compare!

"Florence!" Grandmother cries.

I resume my slow, careful descent, despite her protests that I am taking too long. When I reach her, her breaths come too quickly.

I put a hand on her shoulder. "You're all right, Grandmother. I'm here now."

Her eyes meet mine, and some of the panic seems to leave her. "This is more burdensome than I imagined."

"Don't you always say that life is harder than we predict it will be? Now, let's get you unstuck."

Before I can aid Grandmother, I must secure myself. I can't use Mr. Anderson's rope—it's strung through the bolts. Instead, I slip my own rope through the nearest bolt and tie it around my waist. I stare down at the thin, twisted line, suddenly unable to let go of the bigger rope. Will this hemp rope we made hold me? Of course it will. Sally Ann and Johnny would never let me fall. I test my knot before letting go of Mr. Anderson's line.

Taking a stable stance on my good foot and with my hands now free, I push on Grandmother's boot as she twists her foot. Together we pry and pull until her boot works loose, then I collapse against the rock. My foot buckles unexpectedly, and pain shoots through my ankle. Try as I might to hide my wince, Grandmother sees.

"You're hurt," she says.

I cannot look at her. My ankle throbs.

"There's no hiding it now. Can you go on?" Grandmother asks.

"I have to try."

"Yes, you do. I'll stay here."

The thought of anyone lingering on this smooth face is terrifying.

"We'll go together," I say, untying my rope from the bolt and settling it over my shoulder.

Her gaze follows Mr. Anderson's rope up the curve of rock where it disappears. Then she looks back at me. "I suppose we shall."

I convince her to go first but follow closely so that I can help if her foot gets stuck again. Our progress—with her methodical pace, my injury, and four achy arms between us—remains slow on the steep ascent, and each eyebolt gained is a victory.

I am doing it!

I'm making my dream come true—one slippery, painful step at a time.

My arms burn with exertion, but the feeling focuses my attention. When Grandmother pauses to catch her breath, I find a small lip to rest my toes on, keeping a firm hold on Mr. Anderson's rope until she starts up again. Before long, the slope begins to lessen, and the pain in my ankle subsides. I no longer require as hard of a grip on the rope, and I can see Father waiting for us not thirty feet away. Then the rope stops altogether—the final bolt has been reached.

We've made it!

I throw my arms around my grandmother, and she embraces me in return.

"Thank you," I say.

"We have done it together, Florence."

Father steps forward and takes Grandmother's arm. "Steady, Florantha," he says. "It's easy from here."

He is right. Beyond him is an open space broad enough for a stagecoach to drive in wide circles. I limp to the middle of the expanse and lie down, taking in the vast cloudless blue sky overhead. If not for the cool rock beneath me, I would feel as if I were flying.

I linger on the rock for a good while before making my way to where Father and Grandmother are looking out across the Valley. They are standing far back from where the rock drops away into a void, but the temptation to approach the brink is too strong for me to deny. I stop a body's length from the edge and lie down on my stomach. Inch by inch, I drag my way forward, pausing as my fingertips fold over the granite lip. A nervous laugh escapes me, but after all that has happened to arrive at this point, these last few inches will not stop me. Finally, my eyes just gain the precipice.

Oh, how far I've come!

Below is Mirror Lake and the tiny dance floor. Glacier Point, the mound of Sentinel Dome, and the mighty profile of El Capitan all lie to the west. To the east, and the Sierra Nevada high country beyond, many more peaks dot the horizon. And here I am, on Half Dome, in the center of it all. From this place, I can see where two glaciers joined as one to carve out my beloved Yosemite and the forested foothills of this range rolling into California's great fertile valley. From here, everything looks different.

Even I do.

I ease backward until the edge is far enough away and then stand. I am pulling *Zanita* out of my satchel just as Father comes to my side.

"What's that?" he says.

I hold the book out for him to see.

His eyebrows pinch together. "And you've read that, I take it?"

"I have."

"Then you know it's melodramatic and not worthy of any literary acclaim."

"In the end, Zanita falls off Half Dome," I say.

"And yet, here you are."

"Yes." I beam. "Here I am."

Then I throw the book over the edge. It drops like a stone, and then the pages start to flutter, like a bird desperate to take flight.

Father's eyes follow the book as it falls and disappears out of sight. "I suppose I'll have to buy another copy," he says dryly.

"You just claimed it was terrible! Besides, that was Mrs. Snow's copy. I stole it."

His laughter is carried away by a sudden gust of wind. "Come, Floy. Let's get your grandmother down."

I do not miss that he calls me by my preferred name. My heart cannot be any fuller. "I'll be there shortly."

He kisses my forehead and leaves me alone.

I touch the bracelet at my wrist. Whatever the future holds for me and my friends, whatever places we'll call home, nothing can replace this summer of friendship and dreams.

Then I reach into my satchel and bring out a small rock—the very rock I'd almost given Willie not seven months ago. Until I'd stood at the bottom end of Mr. Anderson's rope, sensing the heartbeat of Half Dome, I'd never considered that my rock was actually a tiny piece of the mountain of my dreams. A mighty glacier carried it several miles and deposited it thousands of years ago not far from El Capitan, where I'd found it. Maybe it was waiting for me all that time.

In a few weeks, when my family returns to San Francisco for the winter, I shall no longer harbor fears of losing myself. I will return to Yosemite, even if I cannot say when that may be.

I do not need a rock to remind me of that.

I wedge the rock into a slim crack at my feet, satisfied that it—like me—is home now. Then I take in the view one last time, and my heart feels as vast as the mountain range before me. I am no longer the tragic heroine in someone else's novel.

I am Floy Hutchings, and my story has just begun.

Adventuring Like a Modern-Day Floy

FLOY HUTCHINGS'S YOSEMITE is vastly different from the Yosemite modern visitors experience, and her way of interacting with the natural world—exploring alone, for example—was a product of her unique upbringing. While acceptable for 1876, a number of Floy's choices are not considered best practice for adventuring in wild places today. As you head out to explore, use these guidelines to stay safe and to protect the land for future adventurers.

- Tell someone where you are going and when you plan to be back.
- Hike with a partner or in a group.
- Pick a trail suitable for the abilities of all hikers.
- Wear sturdy footwear and carry equipment, including clothing, water, a flashlight, and snacks appropriate for the terrain and length of the hike.
- Stay on designated trails.
- Take any trash out with you.
- Leave nature as you find it. Take pictures, instead of natural objects or cultural artifacts. And never throw anything off a cliff!

Author's Note

CALL ME FLOY IS A WORK OF FICTION, but Florence "Floy" Hutchings was a real person—the first European American child born in Yosemite, on August 23, 1864. Floy did freely roam the Valley, an unusual pursuit for a girl of her times but fitting for her unique upbringing. When not exploring, she spent her time in the company of the well-educated, intellectual adults her father, James Hutchings, hosted in his hotel. Her young companions included her two siblings, a dozen or so European American children, and the children of indigenous people who called the Valley home. Most of Floy's adventurous but short life took place in Yosemite, with some winters spent in San Francisco.

James Hutchings is arguably as important to Yosemite's history as is the famous writer and environmentalist John Muir. Born in England, Hutchings arrived in California at the end of the Gold Rush and worked as a miner. After his first visit to the Valley in 1855, his attention became fixed on Yosemite and its promotion. He and Muir are often painted as nemeses, but Hutchings's love for Yosemite certainly rivaled Muir's, and while Muir dedicated his life to the idea of national parks, it was Hutchings who dedicated his life to championing Yosemite.

Hutchings met Elvira, his first wife, while staying at

Florantha Sproat's San Francisco boardinghouse. Elvira was quite unhappy in Yosemite, and they eventually separated around the time of this story. Her mother, Florantha, stayed with Hutchings and the children, both in Yosemite and in San Francisco, for many years. A few years younger than her sister, Floy, Gertrude "Cosie" Hutchings was also an adept horsewoman. She continued to visit Yosemite periodically and even adventured alone in the high country in her eighties. William Yosemite Hutchings, born with a spinal deformity, worked as a cabinetmaker in the Valley.

Floy's story hints at just a sliver of the history of the indigenous people who lived, and continue to live, in the Yosemite area. Likewise, this short note can do little justice to both the complex story of the people—Ahwahneechee, Yosemite, Paiute, Miwok, Mono, and Yokuts—who historically lived in Yosemite Valley and the impact of its "discovery" by European Americans. In fact, for many years, indigenous communities across California were deliberately targeted for destruction by local, state, and federal governments as well as by individuals. Educators looking for accurate, contemporary curricula to teach indigenous history might explore the History Project at the University of California, Irvine.

In all likelihood, Floy held positive views of the indigenous people she knew. Sally Ann Dick, born in the Sierra foothills at her family's wintering grounds, was about five years younger than Floy. While Sally Ann's age has been changed for this story, in reality their age difference would not have mattered. There were few children in the Valley to play with, and Floy and Sally Ann were kindred souls—free spirits who loved to ride horses. Sally Ann became a respected basket maker, just like her mother, May. Tom, a Paiute, met Hutchings soon after his arrival in the Valley. Tom assisted Hutchings in a seed-distribution business and also worked as the Valley postman. The two formed a strong bond—Tom eventually took Hutchings's last name, and Hutchings mentions him in the acknowledgments of his 1886 book, *In the Heart of the Sierras*.

In 2018, more than four million people visited Yosemite National Park. In 1876, the year *Call Me Floy* takes place, visitation totaled around 1,900 people. The Yosemite Valley during Floy's life was vastly different from what it is today. At the time in this book, indigenous communities lived seasonally at village sites used for centuries. They, along with people from Italy; China; Mexico; and England, such as Hutchings; and Scotland, like Muir and George Anderson, supported Valley tourism through work as stonemasons, road builders, packers, horse wranglers, launderers, cooks, fishermen, blacksmiths, and hoteliers. Most of the characters in Floy's story are based on real people.

George and Isabella Leidig raised eleven children while maintaining their hotel at the base of Sentinel Rock. Albert and Emily Snow ran La Casa Nevada on the way to Half Dome and the Tuolumne high country; their register serves as a valuable visitor record. Billy Hurst operated his saloon for sheepherders and cowhands and did climb Half Dome just a few weeks after Floy completed her ascent. George Monroe was a master at the reins who drove three presidents by stagecoach into Yosemite Valley. Manuel Flores's parents operated a laundry in Yosemite Village; he spent summers working as a guide. The children of these people did not attend school until 1875, when the first Yosemite Valley School was established. An early student register lists the name "Johnny Boitano." In the 1880s, children of the indigenous community were invited to attend the school, a sign of increased assimilation into pioneer life. The school still operates in Yosemite National Park today and is located on the north side of the Valley near the site of Hutchings's old cabin.

John Muir makes minor appearances in *Call Me Floy*, but for a short time he saw Floy almost daily. In 1869, a thirty-one-year-old Muir arrived in the Valley to work for Hutchings. For two years, Muir cut lumber from fallen trees at Hutchings's mill on Yosemite Creek, living in an attached room he built over the water. He was friendly with the Hutchings children, sharing his milk and bread when Elvira's dieting fads left them hungry. By this time, Floy was five years old and had already developed her adventurous spirit, but Muir's own ramblings probably had some influence on her. Together, Floy and Muir were the inspiration for the novel *Zanita: A Tale of the Yosemite* by

Thérèse Yelverton, published in 1872. While the main character—based on Floy and loved by all, as she was—did fall off Half Dome, there is no historical evidence that Floy felt disturbed by the novel and the heroine's demise.

Floy's passionate dream of climbing Half Dome is my creation for the novel, but she did indeed make the climb in 1876 with her father, grandmother, George Anderson, and a Mr. Hamilton from San Francisco. As part of the sixth party to ever reach the summit, Floy was roughly the seventeenth person—and the youngest—to climb the peak; her father was the thirteenth on a previous climb.

In the years following her ascent, Floy returned to the Valley seasonally until her father's appointment to serve as Yosemite's Guardian, an early version of a park ranger, allowed a permanent homecoming. In her teenage years, she worked as a guide for groups of adventurous women and as a caretaker for the newly built chapel, until her unexpected death at only seventeen. Reports of how it happened offer conflicting stories. In an interview conducted more than sixty years later, Cosie stated that her sister had died while hiking when a rock dislodged from above and struck her in the head. However, the newspaper obituary, printed days after her death on September 26, 1881, states that Floy became suddenly ill after falling in cold water. Might she have caught pneumonia? It's possible.

What we do know for certain is that Floy's influence continues to live on in Yosemite today. Mount Florence, the tenth-highest peak in the national park, was named for Floy shortly after she died; it can be seen from Glacier Point. The Yosemite Chapel, whose floorboards she lovingly swept, still stands, not far from the site of Hutchings's hotel. Though no longer maintained as an orchard, a handful of the apple and pear trees her father planted more than 150 years ago continue to bear fruit each year; look for them on the eastern edge of Yosemite Creek. Floy's grave is in the Yosemite Valley Cemetery, near those of her father, George Anderson, and her friend Sally Ann. And her spirit surely lives on in the young people who love nature and Yosemite as she did.

To create this story, I read many primary sources, including tourist accounts, travel guides, and newspaper articles from the period of Floy's life, not to mention a wealth of publications that Hutchings printed and distributed himself. That said, authors of historical fiction often condense time to create a stronger story. For example, the tunnel tree in the now Tuolumne Grove of Giant Sequoias was not completed until 1878. Historical names also presented a challenge. In the 1870s, Half Dome was widely known as South Dome; I chose to use the name most readers know best. Neither the term *Native Americans* nor *American Indians* was in use at the time. Texts published by Floy's father and others predominately use *Indian* or *indian*. In his 1877 book, *Tribes of California*, the ethnographer Stephen Powers used the spelling *Awani* to refer to the indigenous group then living in Yosemite. This story reflects these historical usages.

The best resources for those who want to know more are the many books on Yosemite written by Shirley Sargent. Of specific relevance to Floy, consider reading *Enchanted Childhoods* and *Pioneers in Petticoats*.

As for me, Yosemite is one of my heart homes. In my twenties, I lived and worked in the national park for close to eight years and enjoyed many long days beneath granite walls and thundering waterfalls just as Floy did. This story, along with my Yosemite picture book, *The Sequoia Lives On*, is essentially a love song to that inspiring landscape and the people who came before me. I'm lucky to have explored many favorite, secret places, as no doubt Floy did. And yet, as of this writing, I have not climbed Half Dome! Blazes! Connecting with Floy has inspired me to make my own attempt, and perhaps I can make history as the five-millionth person (give or take) to ascend the mighty mountain. See you at the top!

Acknowledgments

WRITING A NOVEL is like climbing a mountain. It is accomplished step by painstaking step. While writing Floy's story, I was lucky enough to have the guidance of mentors, the company of friends, and the love of family as I slogged my way to the top of my own metaphorical Half Dome.

To my team at Yosemite Conservancy: Adonia Ripple, thank you for asking me to write a picture book on giant sequoias. I wouldn't be here today if you hadn't. Nicole Geiger, thank you for sharing your wisdom. Your trust in me and encouragement during the tricky bits made all the difference.

To my Yosemite historians: Jim Snyder, your love of history inspired my own. Floy could not have come to life without you. Pete Devine, there is no better partner with whom to explore our beloved Valley. To my editorial team: Debbie Carton, Jennifer Stanton, Emily Dayhoff, Hazel Galloway, Patricia Callahan, and Christine Ma, thank you for your honesty and suggestions. To Melissa Brown and Zeke Peña, thank you for bringing a modern aesthetic to Floy's story. And a special appreciation to Joe Dolan and Dean Tonenna: I am indebted to you for your critical readings.

To my writing community: Katie Cullinan and Anne Brentan, thank you for ten years of writing. Here's to ten more, and to the day we actually drink tea together in real life. Hunter Liguore, this story is the synthesis of what I learned in your historical fiction class. And your editing class. And your other editing class. Lesley MFA community, I couldn't have had a better jump start to the writing life. Jackson Hole Kidlit Critique, thank you for connecting me with local writers (and new running partners).

To my Jackson friends: Many thanks to all for childcare and for understanding when I had yet another weekend of revision.

To my family: Mom and Dad, your love and support helped me realize every identity I ever desired. I feel limitless because of you. Jen, thank you for teaching me to embrace the risks in being an artist. You inspire me. Karsten, you may not (yet) love reading as much as I do, but your zest for life and for wild places kept me sane while writing. I'm lucky you chose me to be your mom. Chris, storms can thwart any mountain climb, and as I'm rather competent at generating my own storms, your equanimity and optimism have been vital in my completing Floy's story. You never balk at stolen weekends (or anything I ask for) and let me talk nonstop about ~~fictional people~~ everything. I love you.